*"How do yo...*  *whispered.*

"What do you me... ...wn voice. Deep. Husky. Sexy.

Drawing back, Jake gave her a lazy smile. "This was your idea. How do you like it...a little rough?" He gripped her waist and forced her back until she was against the bedroom wall, then he pushed his tongue between her lips.

Just as quickly, he withdrew to lightly nibble the side of her mouth, releasing her to cup her face in his hands, giving a gentle but very satisfying kiss.

"Or slow and tender?"

It took Tori a moment to catch her breath. "Well... if you *really* want to spend the night analyzing the situation, we should put our clothes back on," she quipped, dipping a couple of fingers into his boxers.

"I've gotta admit, Ms. Whitford——" his gaze surveying her lips, then her breasts "——you turned out mighty fine."

She kneaded the muscles along his upper arms, ran her palms down to his backside. When she reached for, then stroked, his erection, she replied, "Well, Mr. Conners, I'm happy to say the same about you...."

# Blaze™

Dear Reader,

This book will always remind me of my recent move. Yes, I know I said that before, and for four years I actually stayed put. Pretty good for me. But then my sister decided to move here from Hawaii, and while helping her look for a place I discovered this awesome model town house nearby. In six days my house was sold and there was no turning back.

It didn't matter that the new house was late on completion or that this book was due—I had to plow ahead, grumbling to my sister that it was all her fault. I even named the heroine's sister after the sales rep, and the heroine's last name is the name of the model of home I purchased. Not to mention that two of the guys her mom tries to fix her up with are named for the other two town house models! Oh well, the new place is finally finished! And this book is *done* and I sure hope you enjoy it!

Did I say what a peach my editor is? Kathryn was wonderfully patient through the entire ordeal. Even though it took an act of Congress to reach me.

*Debbi Rawlins*

## Books by Debbi Rawlins

HARLEQUIN BLAZE

13—IN HIS WILDEST DREAMS
36—EDUCATING GINA
60—HANDS ON
112—ANYTHING GOES…

# HE'S ALL THAT

*Debbi Rawlins*

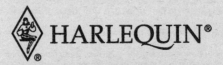

HARLEQUIN®

TORONTO • NEW YORK • LONDON
AMSTERDAM • PARIS • SYDNEY • HAMBURG
STOCKHOLM • ATHENS • TOKYO • MILAN • MADRID
PRAGUE • WARSAW • BUDAPEST • AUCKLAND

This is for my sister, Earlette.
I can't wait for you to get here.

And for the real Mallory.
Your humor and wit made the wait tolerable.
Thank you.

ISBN 0-373-79147-X

HE'S ALL THAT

Copyright © 2004 by Debbi Quattrone.

This edition published by arrangement with Harlequin Books S.A.

® and TM are trademarks of the publisher. Trademarks indicated with
® are registered in the United States Patent and Trademark Office, the
Canadian Trade Marks Office and in other countries.

www.eHarlequin.com

**Printed in U.S.A.**

# 1

"ISABELLE, bring me my social calendar along with another pot of tea."

Victoria Whitford sighed at the boorish way her mother spoke to their longtime housekeeper. The woman was practically part of the family, for God's sake. She'd been ready with a Band-Aid the first time Tori had scraped her knee.

"Thank you," Tori added for her mother, not that Marian Whitford noticed the subtle criticism.

Isabelle smiled. "Would you like some vanilla wafers with your tea, Tori?"

"My God, don't call her that horrid name. It's Victoria."

"Sorry, Mrs. Whitford." Isabelle scurried out of the sitting room, her sensible black shoes treading lightly over the polished wood floors.

"I like Tori, Mother."

"That is not the name your father and I gave you."

"Nevertheless, I suggest you get used to it."

Her mother glared in disbelief. Her sister Mallory laughed.

Marian turned on her older daughter. "What do you find so amusing?"

She looked away and brought the martini glass to her lips.

"Don't look away while I'm speaking to you."

Tori waited for her sister to make a snide remark. But the only sign of her old defiance was a slight lift of her chin as she turned her attention back to their mother.

"Put that glass down. What have I told you about drinking so early in the day?"

With a sinking heart, Tori watched Mallory obey. Not that she approved of her sister's drinking, something that she'd done quite a bit since Tori had gotten home three days ago, but she hated to see her spirited sister look so broken.

Having been away for seven years had really shed a different light on the home front. Even though Tori had spent half her life at boarding school, when she'd returned home for holidays and summers she'd never noticed her mother's domineering attitude. Of course Tori had always been the obedient daughter and seldom her mother's target.

"Is that couch new?" she asked, wanting to change the subject, yet seriously interested in the answer.

Her mother reared her head back, her carefully made-up blue eyes widening. "That piece belonged to your great-grandmother. It's been in the family for generations."

"Oh." It was ugly. Burgundy velvet, trimmed with

gold, obviously an antique, probably valuable. Tori hated it. "Is it comfortable?"

"For God's sake, you don't sit on it."

Tori froze just as she swiveled, ready to plant her fanny on the diminutive settee. "Silly me," she murmured, and Mallory hid a smile.

Isabelle appeared with a tray and as she poured the tea, Tori wandered over to the window overlooking the south garden, breathtaking as always with tiers of award-winning lavender and pink roses and crawling jasmine.

The Whitford mansion was beautiful, having been featured in *Arch Digest* twice, but Tori had always liked the gardens the best. They soothed her, helped her feel connected to the world. She missed them while she'd been away, sadly, more than she'd missed her family.

Of course it wasn't the flowers that had initially caught her interest. Jake Conners had done that. The gardener's son had the body of a god and when he'd take his shirt off, even her prepubescent heart would flutter like crazy. She wondered whatever happened to him. He was at least five years older. Probably married with two kids, living halfway across the country by now.

"Victoria?"

She turned to her mother. Fifty-eight years old and not a crease on her face, not a strand of gray glistening from her perfect blond bob.

"You're not to make any plans this week without checking with me first," she said opening her leather-bound appointment book. "We have a very full schedule."

Out of the corner of her eye, movement in the garden caught Tori's attention. She moved her head for a better look and squinted at the figure holding the shovel.

Her breath caught.

It couldn't be...

"Victoria, are you listening to me?"

"Yes, Mother, I heard every word." She changed windows for a better angle, and stared in giddy disbelief.

"For heaven's sake, Victoria." Her mother came up behind her, moved the heavy cream-colored drape aside and followed Tori's gaze with disdain. "Don't even think about dallying with the Conners boy."

"My God, it really is Jake?"

Mallory joined them at the window. "Yummy, isn't he? I haven't seen him for ages."

"You two disgust me." She let go of the drape. "Step away from there before he sees you ogling him like a couple of schoolgirls." She returned to the sofa and her appointment book as if the matter were settled. "This Saturday we have dinner with the Radcliffs. You do remember their son, Bradley, don't you, Victoria?"

"How could I forget? The first time we met he tried to impress me by reciting the entire Gettysburg Address." Tori shuddered. "And that was as interesting as he got."

"That may be so but he's executive vice president of Radcliff Enterprises now. Rumor has it he'll take over when his father retires in two years. You could do much worse, Victoria."

She gave her mother a mischievous smile. "You're listening to the rumor mill these days?"

She looked up from her appointment book. "I had lunch with Claire Radcliff." Annoyance flashed in her eyes. "I don't much care for your attitude since you've been home, young lady. Even your father commented after dinner last night."

Yeah, right. Like he'd notice anything that didn't concern Whitford Industries' bottom line. Which was fine with Tori. At least he didn't interfere in her life. Of course Mother effectively managed that. As if Tori didn't fully understand what was expected of her.

"Okay, so what else besides dinner with the Radcliffs?"

"Let's see..." Her mother adjusted her reading glasses and then perused the appointment book. "Ah, yes, we have another dinner with Sela and Jonathon Matthews and their son Nelson. That would be on Friday at the Club."

As she listened to her mother drone on, Tori's gaze drifted back out the window. Jake had moved to the climbing jasmine and she could barely get a glimpse of him but her mind filled in the details of his slim hips, narrow waist, broad shoulders. The way his tanned skin glistened with exertion.

Suddenly it didn't seem like a dozen years ago

when she'd stood at her bedroom window, hiding behind the white lace curtains that matched her canopy bed. If he'd known she was there, staring and holding her breath, he'd never let on. He'd just kept digging or pruning, muscles rippling along his shoulders and back, and sending her poor pounding heart into overdrive.

Once when he'd been working on the pond off the solarium, she'd had to sneak into Mallory's room in order to watch him. Isabelle had caught her sitting on the windowsill. She'd only smiled. Never said a word to anyone.

"Well, I see this is a wasted afternoon." Her mother tapped the tip of her Montblanc pen to get Tori's attention.

"You're right, Mother," Tori said, leaving the window and crossing the room, away from her mother and Mallory. "Let's do this some other time."

"Victoria!"

She didn't hesitate, but headed for the staircase. Excitement slid over her like honey on a hot biscuit. She had to write her e-mail friends.

To: The Gang at Eve's Apple
From: Angel@EvesApple.com
Subject: Hot damn!
Color me happy. I finally get it—what you all have been going on about. Because...tada...I found him!!!! My man to do has been under my nose. Well, not for quite a while. I actually just saw him again after about eight years, but I digress... I'll

start from the beginning— His name is Jake and he's got the body of Adonis. No kidding. He could be in a calendar or a centerfold or something. Anyway—

Tori stopped typing, reviewed what she'd written and frowned. Maybe using Jake's name wasn't such a good idea. None of the girls knew who she was. They only knew her by her screen name "Angel." And of course they were scattered across the country. She knew a couple of them were from the East Coast and it was highly unlikely their paths would ever cross, but still if anyone ever linked her to this confession...

She shuddered at the thought of her mother's reaction. Altering a few minor details wouldn't change the story. Quickly she went back and changed Jake's name to simply J before she continued.

When I was about twelve, I first saw J. He was our neighbor's gardener's son and as I mentioned a whole five years older than me. God, I couldn't stop staring at him. At that age I didn't know why I'd gotten that soft squishy feeling inside every time I saw him, especially with his shirt off <g>. Anyway, my mother had forbidden me to "fraternize" with him and since I was an obedient daughter in those days I never said a word to him. Only worshiped him from afar. <major sigh>

Today I saw him again. Shirt off, looking extremely buff. Frankly, I'm surprised he still lives around here. Oh, hell, something just occurred to me. I hope he's not married. Well, better go see if he's wearing a ring.

Oh, question. How direct should I be? I don't want to turn him off or anything, but I want to make sure he knows it's only about sex. No sleeping in late and reading the paper together. No meeting the folks. Just sex. Should I lay it on the line right off the bat? Most men would jump at the chance at no-strings-attached sex, right?

Really anxious to hear from you all. Have to admit I'm a little nervous. Okay, my hands are shaking here. Write to me soon, okay?

Thanks! You guys are the best.

Angel

Tori signed off, closed her laptop and hurried to the window. She couldn't see him, but an old red truck was parked in the back that had to belong to him.

She stopped at her vanity mirror to check her reflection, added a touch of color to each cheekbone, calculatedly tousled her hair and then headed for the back servants' stairs that ended up off the pantry. That way she wouldn't run into her mother. She doubted Marian Whitford had ever even seen the kitchen.

Mission accomplished, Tori got down the stairs and through the kitchen without seeing a soul. But just as she got to the back door, Mallory entered from the dining room.

Her sister gave her a wry smile. "Where are you going?" Her smile widened, her gaze straying out the kitchen window toward the truck. "Let me guess."

Tori sighed. "Mallory..."

"Hey, if I could I'd go for it." She opened the pantry door and dug around the canisters of flour and sugar and then pulled out a bottle of gin.

Tori frowned.

"I'm sick of mom getting on my case," Mallory said, shrugging, as she poured a drink. "What she doesn't know won't hurt her."

Tori hesitated. She and her sister had just started to get close before Tori had gone off to college. She didn't want to stir anything up but she couldn't keep her mouth shut, either. "You do seem to be drinking a lot."

"You would, too, if you were married to Richard." Mallory sighed and then took a long sip. "Go find Jake before he leaves."

Tori's chest tightened. The resignation in Mallory's voice and face really got to her. But there wasn't much more she could say right now. Later, away from the house, they'd have a talk. When Mallory turned away and headed toward the dining room, Tori escaped out the back door.

As soon as she rounded the hydrangea bush, she saw that the truck was gone. She thought she heard an engine and hurried toward the driveway. Jake stood outside the truck's open door, pulling on his shirt, while the other man loaded shovels and other equipment onto the bed.

Tori's mouth went dry as she stared at the stretch of taut skin across his belly until he pulled the shirt hem down. Swallowing hard, she moistened her lips and touched her hair. The other man climbed in, and Jake got behind the wheel and started to reverse the truck before she could get her wits about her.

She rushed toward them but apparently he didn't see her. He stopped briefly and then shifted into Drive and started to roll forward just as she got to the back of the truck. Tongue-tied suddenly, she hesitated. She hadn't actually spoken to him before. He probably didn't even know her name. What the hell should she say?

He started to pull away.

"Jake!"

Slowly he turned to her, glancing out of the open window, his dark eyes not at all surprised as if he'd seen her coming, his lips barely curving into a smile. "Hello, Victoria," he said casually, as if they'd just talked yesterday.

She smiled back.

And then he drove down the driveway and through the double white gates without looking back.

VICTORIA WHITFORD.

Shit, he almost hadn't recognized her. When had she gotten back?

Another driver blared his horn at Jake as he pulled his father's old truck onto the highway and narrowly missed the white Honda.

Hector jumped. "You okay, *amigo?*"

"Yeah. I forgot this relic doesn't have any guts. My father should've gotten rid of it years ago."

"No way. Not him." Hector stuck his arm out the window and hit the outside of the passenger's door. "This is good enough. He doesn't go any farther than the Whitfords' or the grocery store these days."

Jake shook his head. He hated that his father continued to work when he could retire. Why he even wanted to work for people like the Whitfords was a mystery. Yet he'd meticulously tended their garden for over twenty years, and this was the first time he'd so much as missed a day's work. Even with two slipped discs and a pinched nerve, he probably would have tried to make it if Jake hadn't caved in and agreed to take over for two weeks.

He could have trusted Hector with the Whitfords' grounds. Jake often sent him over to help his dad under the pretense that business was slow and Jake needed to give the man work. But if his father got wind of it, the old man would be climbing into his overalls and work boots in seconds flat.

*"Amigo?"*

Jake glanced at Hector.

"I think you missed the turn."

"What?" Jake realized he'd just passed his dad's street and cursed under his breath.

Hector chuckled. "Who was the *chica?* An old girlfriend, maybe?"

"Who?"

"The one back there that's made you *loco*."

Jake snorted. "Victoria Whitford? I wasn't even thinking about her," he said and ignored Hector's disbelieving grunt.

"I think she wanted you to stop."

"I doubt it." Hell, he didn't think she even knew his name. She and her sister had always been off-limits. Even as kids they'd had no contact.

His father had forbidden him to so much as speak to either of the girls. Not that Jake had anything in common with them. Most of the time they were off at boarding school. He'd been lucky to keep his ass in River Oaks High without getting thrown out.

"Me, I would have stopped." Hector slicked back his hair and inspected his swarthy, handsome face in the side mirror. "She looked *muy* fine."

Jake smiled. Yeah, she looked good all right. But even Hector's impressive reputation with the ladies at Huey's Bar and Grill wouldn't help him get an invite to the Whitfords' front door.

"I don't remember seeing her before," Hector said. "Only the other one, the blonde."

Jake used the gravel road running around to the back of his father's cottage. The same small, two-bedroom house Jake and his older sister had practically grown up in after their mother died. The place belonged to the Whitfords. Just like most everything on the block. "I don't know. And I sure as hell don't care."

Hector eyed him curiously as they got out of the truck. "For someone who doesn't know her, *amigo,* it sure sounds like you don't like her."

Jake didn't miss the irony of Hector's observation. The truth was, it felt damn good to walk away from a Whitford. Not kowtow to them like his father had done for the past twenty years. But damn if he wasn't curious about what Victoria had wanted. And damn if Hector wasn't right. She looked mighty fine.

# 2

TORI ERASED THE FIRST sentence to her e-mail buddies. It sounded too whiny and undignified. Pathetic, actually. Kind of like when Melissa Hastings had announced to their sorority house that she'd had the hots for Charles Zimmer III, and he overheard and transferred out of their mutual classes. Everyone had gone overboard pretending they hadn't noticed the snub.

She adjusted the pillows behind her, pulled the 800-thread-count sheet over her bare legs and then returned her attention to her laptop. First, none of her cohorts knew who she was, and second, this wasn't the same situation. Jake hadn't really snubbed her. He simply hadn't realized she wanted to chat.

They didn't even know each other. So how the hell was she going to get him in bed?

For reinforcement, she scrolled back to the encouraging e-mail she'd received from Taylor.

To: Angel
From: Taylor@EvesApple.com
Subject: Congratulations!!!

How cool!! I'm so happy for you. Great feeling when you know he's the one, huh? Reminded me of how excited I was when I first saw Ben again after all those years. Got me all tingly.

Anyway, the thing you have to ask yourself is what do you have to lose. And is it worth it? Obviously, I'd advise being direct and let him know what you want since it worked for me. If for some alien, bonehead reason he turns you down, yes, your pride will sting. And then you'll get over it. But if you don't go for it, and he gets away, you'll kick yourself until the next millennium.

I'd bet anything he's been as curious about you as **YOU ARE** about him. Go, girl! Strike while the iron is hot. I can't wait to hear about what happens! My fingers and toes are crossed for you.
Love and kisses,
Taylor, who's sending good vibes your way

Smiling at Taylor's enthusiasm, Tori still wished she'd heard from the other girls, too. Of course Taylor would be enthusiastic after her fairy-tale marriage to Ben. He'd been her first and best sexual experience. She'd wanted to get him out of her system so she could move on with her life. They'd ended up at the altar.

Great for them. But that wasn't how Tori wanted her chapter to end. She really and truly just wanted a fling. Eventually she'd get married. But Jake wasn't suitable husband material.

After sending Taylor a personal thank-you, she

went back to review her e-mail, and see how it read after having deleted the first sentence.

To: The Gang at Eve's Apple
From: Angel@EvesApple.com
Subject: Initial Contact
Okay, so this isn't as easy as it sounded. My first attempt at engaging J in conversation ended up with me running after his truck like a moron. He didn't stop. Just said hello, and then drove off. It wasn't as if I had time to piss him off. Besides, I don't really know the guy.

Oh God, maybe he is married. Of course I'll back off. But I'll wallow in self-pity for a week. Maybe even a month. I wish you all could see him. I kid you not when I say he's to die for.

I know you all are busy, but I need to move fast (I have an appointment calendar that won't quit) and I'm still floundering a little. Any thoughts?
Wish me luck.
Angel

Tori had just pressed Send when she heard a light knock at her door. Quickly she logged off and closed her computer.

"Victoria? Are you still awake?"

She almost answered her mother but thought better of it and slowly slid beneath the covers. Duty would call soon enough. For now she'd plan her attack and dream about Jake.

"HERE SHE COMES."

Jake used his shirtsleeve to wipe the sweat from his brow and then looked to see what Hector was talking about.

Holding a glass in each hand, Victoria came down the slope from the house. She had on white shorts and a pink shirt. Her legs sure had gotten long in the past few years.

Hector slicked his hair back and gave a low appreciative whistle. Not loud enough for her to hear. Just loud enough to annoy Jake.

He laid the shovel he'd been using against the flagstone retaining wall and pulled off his gloves. "Get the fertilizer out of the truck, will you?"

"Now?" Hector shot him a peeved look.

"Now."

The other man sighed, laid down his shovel and muttered something under his breath as he shot Victoria a parting look before heading for the truck parked a good hundred yards away.

As she got closer, Jake had to force his gaze away from her breasts, the way they bounced with each step and strained against the stretchy fabric. Normally he was a leg man, had a real weakness for slim ankles. But the closer she got, the more he realized there wasn't much about Victoria that didn't interest him.

"Hi," she said, smiling. "Jake, right?"

He nodded, curious as hell. What could she possibly want?

"Of course you've changed. And we've never really formally met..."

"I know who you are, Victoria."

"Tori." Her almond-shaped hazel eyes met his. She had one of those sultry looks that could distract a man if he weren't careful. "That's what my friends call me. Oh, here."

He took the lemonade she offered, and decided not to point out that they weren't friends. "Thanks."

She tilted her head to the side, her eyes holding his captive. "I think this is the first time we've talked, isn't it?"

He nodded, and took a long cool sip as he waited her out.

She moistened her lips, darted a look toward Hector. "How's your dad? I haven't seen him since I've been back."

"He's laid up with a bad back."

"Sorry to hear about that." She smiled. "At least he has you helping him."

"Right." He drained his lemonade just as Hector got back and dropped the bag of fertilizer near Jake's boots.

"For me?" he asked Tori, glancing at the glass she held and giving her one of his lady-killer grins.

She handed him the drink. "I'm Tori."

"Hector."

She smiled politely and then turned back to Jake. "I know you're busy right now. I thought maybe we could meet for a drink later."

Totally floored, he stood there, unable to think of a damn thing to say.

Uncertainty flickered in her face and then she gave a throaty laugh. "Unless you have a wife and a dozen kids waiting for you at home."

Hector laughed. "Jake?"

He gave his friend a warning look. Bad enough she'd taken him by surprise. He didn't need any commentary from Hector. "You can spread the fertilizer now. Start with the pink roses along the path to the pool."

"Sure, boss." Hector gave Tori a parting look before setting the glass aside and heaving the bag of fertilizer over his shoulder.

Jake waited until he was out of earshot and asked, "What time?"

"I'm flexible. Whenever you're done here?"

He looked at his watch. "In about three hours."

"Great." Her lips curved in a sexy smile that made him second-guess his decision. Getting mixed up with a Whitford was begging for trouble.

"Where?"

She glanced toward the house, pristine white and stately against all the lush green oak and magnolia trees. "How about Mustang Sally's? I assume the place is still there."

Her suggestion surprised him. The bar wasn't a place he figured she even knew about much less patronized. And then he got it. She didn't want to be seen with him by anyone she knew.

Amazingly he didn't feel the old anger he would have as a kid. The idea pissed him off but it amused him, too. Hell, he wasn't the one looking for trouble. She was.

TORI GOT TO THE BAR a little early. She sat in the parking lot, listening to a classical CD, her sporty BMW lost in the myriad of huge pickup trucks that filled the lot. She hoped the bar wasn't too noisy so that they could at least talk. Or maybe they shouldn't. Maybe she should hang on to the fantasy of him she'd created in her mind. The one where he obeyed her every command and wanted nothing in return. Right. She'd been surprised enough to discover that his eyes were brown and not blue. Not just brown, actually, but an incredible whiskey-brown, brimming with an intensity that made her fantasies feel tame.

Summers spent gazing out her window, waiting for a glimpse of him, had spawned some juicy stories in her head. Like the time she'd imagined that he climbed the trellis outside her bedroom window and sneaked into her bed. What he'd actually done to her was a little fuzzy at the time since she'd only been about fourteen and rather sheltered, but she remembered he'd been gentle yet demanding, and the coaxing way he'd kissed her, touched her breasts...

Damn, but she wished she'd kept a journal. It would be fun to read now but she'd been too chicken to produce any evidence her mother could find.

A knock on her car window made her jump. She looked into Jake's sexy brown eyes, and then turned the key in the ignition, shutting off the CD and air-conditioning. She grabbed her purse and opened the door. He'd straightened and stepped back, the fly of his faded jeans hitting her eye-level. It looked like that particular fantasy wasn't far off base.

She got out and followed him across the parking lot and into the bar. Most of the tables were already taken, and all the places at the bar.

"Let's try back here," Jake said and led the way past a pair of crowded pool tables and a couple arguing over a game of darts.

In the far corner, it looked as if someone had recently abandoned a table, judging by the empty bottle of beer and the two dollar bills left behind.

"How about over there?" she asked, and moved to claim it before getting an answer.

It was perfect—as far away from the country and western music and the dart players' cursing as they could get. They sat across from one another and a waitress promptly appeared to claim her tip.

She removed the empty bottle, swiped a cursory rag across the top of the table. "What can I get y'all?"

"What have you got on tap?" Tori asked and caught the surprised look Jake gave her.

The waitress named three beers and Tori ordered a Corona.

"Make that two," Jake said, his eyes staying on Tori as the cute blond waitress walked away.

"What?" she finally asked him when he wouldn't look away.

"You always drink beer?"

"No, sometimes I drink wine. I picked up the beer habit in college. Much to my mother's delight."

Now, why had she added that tidbit? She sighed to herself. Obviously Freudian.

"I bet."

"I'm twenty-six. Anything she doesn't like about me, it's time she got over it."

Jake smiled. "You've been away at school all this time?"

"Just about. Four years of undergraduate studies, then one year of graduate school. I took a year off to go to Europe, then went back to school and finished my MBA."

"You don't look like an MBA."

She laughed. "Thank you. I'll definitely take that as a compliment."

"Your parents must be pleased."

Something in the tone of his voice made her uneasy. But she didn't know him well, so she wouldn't judge. Not yet. "Yeah, right," she answered. "They about had cardiac arrests when I told them I wanted to take a year off. They threatened to cut me off and not pay for my last year's tuition."

"You didn't back down?"

"No way. I told them I was tired of school anyway." She leaned back to let the waitress set their beers on the table. When they made eye contact again, he had the most peculiar look on his face.

He smiled. "I take it they gave in."

"After a mega lecture, but yes." She picked up her beer and took a sip. She hadn't expected to be so nervous. Of course she wasn't in the habit of picking up guys. What if he turned her down? She took another sip, realized he was watching her and asked, "What about you?"

He shrugged. "Still in the landscaping business, as you can see."

"Have you been here in Houston the whole time?"

"Do you mean, did I go away to school?"

She didn't understand the hint of sarcasm in his tone but chose to ignore it. "School, traveling, whatever."

He lifted a shoulder. "I went to California for a couple of years, and then Dallas for a short time."

She waited but he didn't seem inclined to give out any more information. "Think you'll stay in Houston?" she finally asked.

"Probably. You?"

The question startled her. "Of course. This is our headquarters."

"Ah, staying in the family business."

Her defenses rose. "Haven't you?"

One side of his mouth lifted as he picked up his beer. "Not exactly."

She watched him tilt the bottle to his lips, wondering why she'd gotten so defensive. She'd be a fool not to keep her hand in Whitford Industries. The company was well-known, the name respected and recognized worldwide. No shame in wanting to stay a part of that success.

He set the beer back on the table, leaving his long, lean fingers wrapped around the bottle, stirring her creative mind and making her forget about anything to do with business.

His nails were surprisingly clean considering the type of work he did, and she easily imagined him running his palms down her bare back, over her breasts.

"So, Tori, why are we here?"

She looked up into those intense dark eyes and wondered what he'd do if she suddenly ran her foot up his leg. She smiled. "Weren't you ever curious? For years the most we did was wave to each other."

His brows rose slightly. "Why do you suppose that was?"

"I wasn't allowed to talk to you," she said, the surprise in his face giving her pause. "I had piano lessons twice a week, ballet three times, and a riding lesson on the weekend. Mother didn't leave me much time for distractions."

One side of his mouth went up in a cocky, almost patronizing way.

"What's that for?"

"What?"

"That look."

"Admit it, your mama didn't want you hanging around with anyone the likes of me."

"That's not true." Indignation rose in her voice. "Of course you were so much older." She paused. "Mother isn't a snob."

"You know her. I don't," he said, shrugging.

Tori sighed. "Okay, sometimes she is. But I don't think—" She broke off, sighing again, unable to defend a position of which she was uncertain. A thin line existed between snobbery and concern for the Whitford name and business.

"Hey, it doesn't matter." He gave her a crooked smile. "You were brave enough to break the barrier. Go where no Whitford has gone before."

"Very funny."

He laughed, reached across the table and covered her hand with his rougher palm. The contact jolted her, and when their eyes met she knew he felt the spark, too. He didn't retreat, but ran the pad of his thumb along the side of her wrist. A small innocuous movement that shouldn't have driven her crazy. She sucked in a breath, and then let it out slowly. His sexy gaze fell to her lips and her mouth went too dry to swallow.

He released her, grabbed his beer and leaned back in his chair. "So, what now?"

Tori took a deep breath. She didn't want to sound too obvious or eager, but no sense wasting any time, either. "Have you eaten? We could have dinner."

He smiled. "I meant, what will you do now that you've finished school?"

"Oh." She gave a breezy laugh, not about to show her embarrassment. "I'll be staying in Houston. I haven't found an apartment yet, though."

He seemed surprised. "You're moving out?"

"Of course. You don't still live with your father, do you?" She paused, recognizing her gaffe. "Not that it would be a bad thing if you did."

"Relax. I don't, but if I did live with my old man, I wouldn't take offense. He's a pretty okay guy."

The look of genuine affection on Jake's face warmed her. Sadly she couldn't say the same for her parents. She loved and respected them, but she didn't like either of them much. Then again, maybe she'd like her father if she'd really gotten to know him. He'd always been working or away on business. Often their schedules clashed. When she'd be home from boarding school for the summer or the occasional weekend, he'd be away. Mostly she wouldn't see him for months at a time.

When she finally slipped out of her musings, she found Jake watching her with open curiosity. His gaze lowered briefly to her breasts, rose to linger on her lips before meeting her eyes. And then it narrowed slightly. "What exactly do you want from me?" he asked finally.

She'd rehearsed all the way over here. Her e-mail buddies were behind her a hundred percent. They'd all voted for the direct approach. She breathed deeply, and said, "Sex."

# 3

THE BAND, just back from a break, started playing an energetic Garth Brooks song when Jake thought he heard Tori say the most bizarre thing. He smiled just thinking about her reaction if he were to tell her what he thought she'd said.

She smiled back and leaned forward until her breasts grazed the table, her clingy V-neck shirt showing off a mouthwatering amount of cleavage. "Is that a yes?"

He sobered quickly. "I didn't hear you."

She straightened, her smile disappearing. "Look, it's either yes or no. You won't hurt my feelings if you aren't interested. But it isn't necessary to toy with me. Because that won't happen."

She'd lied. He had hurt her feelings. It was in her eyes, and the defensiveness of her body language as she crossed her arms and shrunk back against the scarred wood chair.

"Seriously," he said, "I thought I heard you but you couldn't have said what I think you did."

Her mouth began to curve again. "I probably shouldn't have put it that way."

Jake stared back. Man, she had a set of balls on her. Not a bad thing, but damn if he knew what to say.

She blinked, looking a little uneasy, and then picked up her beer and finished it off.

"Okay," he said slowly. "I'm thinking you want to tangle the sheets a little. Am I on the right track?"

She nodded, breaking eye contact to signal the waitress for another beer. She looked back at him, moistened her lips and said, "No strings attached of course."

It wasn't hard to keep a straight face. He was still blown away. "For your benefit or mine?"

"For both of us." She shrugged. "I doubt you're looking for a relationship, and neither am I."

Not with him anyway. He wasn't in her league. No blue blood to pass on to the kiddies. The idea pissed him off. "What makes you think I'm not looking for a relationship?"

Panic crossed her face giving him enormous satisfaction. But then she relaxed and met his eyes with a smugness that ruined his fun. "What are you, about thirty now?" He nodded, and she said, "No wife and kids yet, and when I mentioned the possibility, your friend laughed. Tells me I'm not far off base in my assumption."

*Friggin' Hector.* "Okay, so I've been busy."

"How busy?"

He felt something near the top of his boot. Her foot, he realized. She ran it up his calf over his jeans to his knee, paused and then went to midthigh.

The waitress appeared with two more beers.

Jake straightened when he realized he'd unconsciously been leaning over the table toward Tori. He'd even shifted his hips forward.

"Thanks," he muttered when the woman set the Corona down in front of him, glad he didn't have to look at Tori. She had to be laughing, knowing how she'd gotten to him.

The waitress stuffed her order pad into the back pocket of her jeans and then shifted her tray to her other hand. "Y'all want anything else? We've got chicken wings, hot or mild, or jalapeño poppers. They're pretty good. Not too spicy."

Tori shook her head. "No, thanks. I'm in the mood for something else. How about you?" she asked Jake, the twitch at the corners of her mouth unmistakable.

"I'm good," he told the waitress. "I'll take the check, though."

Tori frowned at him. He wasn't sure what that was about. Maybe she wasn't ready to leave. Maybe she'd been bluffing. Maybe she got off on getting him horny and then kicking him to the curb.

The waitress set the tray on the table and got the order pad out of her pocket. After she ripped off the top sheet and set it in front of Jake, she picked up her tray. "Y'all be good, and come back soon."

Tori tried to grab the check but Jake snatched it first. "I'll take that," she said. "I asked you out, remember?"

He smiled. "How politically correct of you," he

said as he dug into his pocket. "You get it the next time." He flipped through the folded bills, withdrew enough to cover a generous tip, and then looked up. "Assuming there is a next time."

She blinked. "I hope so."

"Good enough." He picked up his beer and tipped the bottle to his lips.

Tori played with the wet napkin under her bottle, lightly sucking in her lower lip, looking as if she had a big decision to make. Or was trying to figure out how to get herself out of this scene gracefully.

Finally she picked up the beer and took a long pull. When she set the bottle down again, her pale pink lips glistened with moisture. Her tongue slipped out to swipe her lower lip, the action sexy as hell. He didn't think it was deliberate, though. In fact, she seemed nervous.

She shook back her hair and smiled. "Okay, where were we?"

"I believe you were playing with my leg."

She sputtered, and then started laughing. "Me?"

"I hope it was you."

"I was minding my own business."

"You mean you didn't do this?"

She jumped when the toe of his boot made contact. "No, I believe my aim was quite a bit lower."

He hadn't meant to land between her thighs, but he wasn't quick to withdraw, either. "Ah, my mistake."

The surprise wore off and she gave him a playful glare as she removed his foot. "Right."

"Damn, I was just getting comfortable."

She laughed. "I'm glad I like you."

"Huh?"

"Having seen you all those years is like following your favorite actor in a TV series and thinking you know him. Then you see him on an interview show and think, oh, my God, he's a geek. Or he's arrogant, or dumber than dirt. Know what I mean?"

"Yeah, I guess."

"I know you saw me over the years, either running to the stables, or even simply leaving in the car. What did you think of me?"

He avoided her probing gaze and flashed back to the time when he'd first seen Tori at a window, hiding behind a curtain where she thought he couldn't see her. She'd watched him for hours, would disappear for a while and then return, sometimes changing windows to track him. She'd been young, too young to interest him, and mostly he'd ignored her.

Except one day, while in a shitty mood after being chewed out by his father for something, Jake had almost gestured to her. He'd wanted to make her aware that he knew she hid at the window. He'd wanted to embarrass her. But at the last moment he'd caught a glimpse of her face and the unhappiness he saw had stopped him cold.

He thought about it for a moment and then said, "I thought you were lonely."

She reared her head back. "What?"

"Sometimes when you stared out your window, you looked—I dunno."

"You saw me at the window—" She briefly covered her mouth. "You never let on."

He shrugged. "You would have been embarrassed."

She laughed softly. "Yeah. So you knew I had a crush on you all along."

"I really didn't think about it," he said and she frowned. He hadn't meant the comment as a dismissal, but if she took it that way so be it. "Look, you want to get out of here. It's getting noisy."

She nodded, and then took a final sip of beer. He let her lead the way, enjoying the snug fit of her low-riding jeans and the seductive sway of her hips. About an inch of skin showed between the hem of her shirt and her waistband. In the center of her back just above the swell of her butt, it looked as if she had a small tattoo, but more likely it was a birthmark. He couldn't imagine that Ms. MBA would have done anything so whimsical or foolish.

They got outside and the blast of hot, humid air made him think again about why he'd chosen to return to Houston. Granted, he generally didn't work outside much anymore, but the heat could be brutal when he did. Damn, he wished Pop would consider retiring. What kind of hold did the Whitfords have over him?

Tori hesitated and turned to him while pushing the hair away from her face and off her neck. "You'd think I'd be used to this heat by now."

"You've been away," he murmured, more interested in the graceful curve of her neck. Normally he liked long hair, but he wanted to see hers swept up. Off her neck and the slope of her shoulders. "Where to now?"

Her startled eyes met his. "Tonight?"

Shit, he should have known. "Yeah."

"I can't tonight. I only meant for us to have a drink. I have a—" She glanced at her watch. "I have to be home within the hour. My mother has plans for me."

"Ah."

She narrowed her gaze. "You think I'm making that up."

"Actually, I think you're chickening out."

Her brows rose. "Tomorrow night. The Westin Hotel at the Galleria. I'll be there by seven."

He dug in his pocket for his keys and led them in the direction of her car. "I'll make the reservation."

"I'll take care of it."

He smiled. "Under Whitford?"

That wiped the smug look off her face. She nibbled her lower lip. "How about...?"

"Use Conners. I have nothing to hide."

They arrived at her car and she turned to face him, her chin lifted in defiance. "I'm not going to debate my desire for privacy with you."

"Good. That'd be a waste of time." He slid an arm around her waist and hauled her against him.

Her mouth opened in surprise and he took full advantage by slipping in his tongue. Her body tensed and then she touched her tongue to his, her ample breasts pressing against his chest as she slid her arms around his neck.

He deepened the kiss and she moaned softly, working her talented fingers into his hair, over his scalp. Cupping her bottom, he pulled her against his erection. She wiggled seductively.

The parking lot was dark and jammed with cars and he thought about opening her car door and laying her down right there. He got as far as the door handle when the nearing sound of laughter stopped him.

Slowly he released her, moving his hands to her hips, gentling the kiss and finally stepping back. She seemed reluctant, but then lowered her hands to her sides and sagged back against the car. One of those two-seater foreign jobs, he realized. No good for what he'd had planned.

They said nothing as the laughing couple stumbled past them. Tori softly cleared her throat. He shifted, trying to adjust the snugness of his jeans. The jangle of keys drew his attention. She'd pulled them out of her purse.

"Thanks for the sneak preview," she said, her mouth curving slowly, her gaze lingering on him as she opened her car door. "I look forward to tomorrow night."

She slid inside, her long, shapely legs molded by the tight denim, holding his attention captive. Reluctantly he closed the door. She started the car and the automatic window smoothly slid down.

"Tomorrow night," he said, and thought about kissing her again but stepped back instead.

"Around seven, right?"

He nodded. "Under what name?"

Her mouth lifted in a mischievous grin. "Lady Chatterly."

The tinted window slid up, obscuring her face, and then she drove away, leaving him in the parking lot with a smile and a hard-on.

TORI MUTTERED A CURSE when she pulled into the driveway and saw the parlor lights on. Of course her mother could have gone to bed and just left them on for her. It was after eleven.

Another light flickered on and Tori sighed as she navigated the circular driveway around to the east garage where she kept her car. She had a good mind to wander out into the garden and make her mother come out and look for her. No way would she put up with a grilling over where she'd been all night. Tomorrow, after she went to the office, no matter how many appointments were on her calendar, she was looking for an apartment.

She could have come home immediately after meeting with Jake. She'd had a half hour to kill before she had to show up at the center. But if she'd gone home for the thirty minutes, she would have had to face her mother's annoying questions.

It was weird to be living at home after being away for seven years. Had she really been that subservient in her youth, or had her mother's domineering gotten worse? Maybe she figured if she could tame Mallory, whipping Tori into shape would be a cinch.

Even Jake had thought Tori had run home to placate her mother. Of course Tori had also led him to that thinking. She didn't know why she hadn't been honest with him, except working at the center, and answering their hot line was something very personal for her. And the truth was, she didn't know Jake.

She laughed to herself as she pulled the car into the garage. She didn't know him...she just wanted to sleep with him. Oh, God...

The door had barely closed behind her when she heard her mother calling from the parlor. Tori thought briefly about running up the servants' stairs but decided not to aggravate her mother any further.

"I'll be right in, Mother," she called and stopped to get a diet Coke out of the fridge. She grabbed an apple, too, since she hadn't eaten dinner.

She took a deep breath, reminding herself to be patient as she entered the parlor.

Her mother purposefully looked at her watch, still on her wrist, even though she had already changed into a satiny peach robe. "Where have you been?"

"Why?"

Her mother's brows arched. "I don't know what's gotten into you since you've been away, Victoria, but your attitude is most unattractive."

Tori sighed. "It's only eleven-fifteen."

Her mother stared in silence for a moment, gave Tori's jeans a disdainful look and then said, "You've been at the center again, haven't you?"

"And that would be a problem?"

"For heaven's sake, Victoria, we give them enough money. You don't need to actually—" She made a sweeping gesture with her hand.

"Get my hands dirty?"

"You know what I mean."

"Yeah." Sighing, Tori popped open the can of cola. "I think I'll take this upstairs with me."

"Victoria."

She stopped, turned around.

"Do not forget about dinner tomorrow night."

"Tomorrow night? Where?"

"Oh, Victoria." Her mother stood, and then turned to plump the pillow she'd been leaning on. "At the Club."

"You didn't tell me about that."

"I most certainly did. We're meeting the Kimballs at seven. They're very important clients of your father's."

Tori's heart sank. "I would have remembered..."

"Not with the way you've been preoccupied lately. Anyway, dress will be casual." She cast a critical gaze over Tori. "Wear your cream linen dress."

"Guess what? They taught me how to dress myself in college."

"I'm not amused, Victoria," her mother called as Tori took the stairs two at a time. "I expect you to be prompt tomorrow. This dinner is very important."

She slipped inside her room, shut the door and sank against it and groaned. Jake would assume she'd chickened out. What the hell was she going to do?

# 4

JAKE IDLY FLIPPED through several more channels and then flung the remote aside. He should have known she wouldn't show up. Yeah, he'd been surprised when he'd shown up early to check in and pay for the room only to find that she'd beat him to it. She'd left a note apologizing that she'd be late, which had bugged him, yet had also been encouraging.

But it was already nine. If he had a brain in his head he'd just leave. Not that he had anything else to do. Bad enough he'd barely been able to concentrate all day. He'd purposely stayed in the office to clear some paperwork off his desk. And what? All he'd managed to do was upset his secretary by screwing up her new filing system.

Muttering over his foolishness for hanging around, he went to the minibar and grabbed another beer out of the fridge. It wasn't as if he hadn't turned down sex before, although admittedly, that wasn't a common occurrence. If he wanted to be totally honest with himself, he kind of got a charge out of a Whitford coming on to him.

He skipped the chair this time and stretched out on the bed, adjusting the pillow behind his neck before resuming his channel surfing. Great hotel but the channel selection sucked. She obviously wasn't going to show. He ought to go home where he could at least catch the end of the Raiders' game.

After taking another pull of beer, he set the bottle on the nightstand and yawned. Screw her. Better that she'd chumped him. She wouldn't even have to know that he'd shown up. He wasn't a toy poodle for her amusement. The sex would probably have been great but it still niggled at him that she wanted to keep him her guilty secret.

She thought he was a gardener...someone beneath her. Granted, he wasn't in her social class, but little did she know that he'd actually...

A light knock at the door had him sitting up. And then he heard a key in the lock and the door opened.

Tori stepped inside the semidark room, her gaze darting first to the television and then to him. She smiled and closed the door behind her. "I'm glad you're still here."

"I was just about to leave."

She quickly sobered. "I'm really sorry about being late. I tried looking for you in the garden today but obviously you weren't there." She laid her purse on the table and moved closer. "I'd totally forgotten about a business dinner I had tonight. I hope you got the note I left at the front desk."

"I got it." He picked up his beer and took another sip before getting to his feet.

"You're angry."

"I wasted two hours waiting for you."

"I'm sorry. Really. I didn't know how else to get a hold of you."

"Did you try my father?"

She blinked, and looked away. "I didn't think of that."

*Bull shit.* He knew damn well she wouldn't have risked letting anyone know they had a date. If you could call their little sex tryst that.

For a moment he thought about calling her on the lie, but what would that solve? Nothing would change. Except it might mean he wouldn't get anything tonight. If he still wanted it...

His gaze went to the hem of her cream dress, where it stopped about three inches above her knee. The style was conservative with a high neck and short sleeves and she shouldn't have looked so damn sexy.

Yeah, he still wanted her, all right.

"Forget it. You're here now," he said, and pulled off his shirt.

Her eyes widened, excitement mixed with fear sparkling from their depths, and she drew a hand up her opposite arm.

The lady wanted a walk on the wild side. Jake smiled. He wouldn't disappoint her.

TORI DREW AN UNSTEADY breath. He didn't look as if he was about to waste any time on small talk or foreplay. She watched him unsnap his jeans, and wished she'd had that brandy her mother had ordered her after dinner. But by the time dessert had arrived, Tori had her purse in hand and excuse to leave the table on her lips.

After she'd fought the downtown traffic, she'd half expected not to find Jake waiting. But here he was, with the best-looking chest in the southern hemisphere.

He shoved the jeans down his thighs and then pulled them off, leaving him in navy-blue boxers. "If you don't want me to mess up that pretty dress of yours, I'd suggest you take it off."

At the deep, suggestive timbre of his voice, a shiver slithered down her spine and she automatically reached behind to find the zipper. His gaze went to her breasts where the linen fabric strained against them and revealed her protruding nipples.

"Need help?"

She looked up when she realized she'd been staring at his fly. Already he was semiaroused which sent her pulse into the danger zone. She fumbled with the zipper, her fingers going numb, so she slowly turned around to accept his help, briefly closing her eyes, anticipating that he might rip the tab off the track.

He didn't, but simply pulled gently until the zipper parted and then he unhooked her bra before she could turn around and do it herself. He slipped the dress off her right shoulder along with the bra strap. She started to turn to face him, but he held her by the shoulders and ran his tongue down the side of her spine.

Her breath caught and she closed her eyes while he slid the dress off her other shoulder. The fabric dropped to her waist where she held it to her tingling skin. The creamy silk bra easily followed so that she was bare to the waist.

Gripping her by the shoulders, he turned her around until their eyes met, briefly, before his gaze lowered to her breasts. She swallowed when he took her wrists and pulled her hands away from the dress. She let go and the pale linen fell to her feet.

He still didn't let go, but lifted his gaze to her face. "How do you like it, Victoria?" he whispered, and then kissed the side of her neck.

"What do you mean?" She barely recognized her own voice. Deep. Husky. Sexy.

He drew back and gave her a lazy smile. "You like it a little rough?" He gripped her wrist tighter and forced her backward until she was against the wall, and then he kissed her hard, pushing his tongue between her lips.

Just as quickly he withdrew, lightly nibbling the side of her mouth, sucking at her lower lip, releasing her wrist to cup her face in his hands and giving her a gentle but very satisfying kiss.

He pulled back, his darkly intense eyes even with hers. "Or slow and tender?"

It took her a moment to catch her breath. "I don't know. I've never—" A glint of triumph in his eyes stopped her. Was he trying to intimidate her? "If you want to spend the night analyzing the situation..." She put a hand on his hip and dipped a couple of fingers into the elastic of his boxers. "Then we might as well put our clothes back on."

His mouth curved in a crooked smile, and before she knew what he was doing, he'd hooked his thumbs in her bikini panties and drew them down her legs, lowering himself so that she felt his warm breath at the juncture of her thighs.

She clutched his shoulder to keep her balance, unsure what he'd do next, nervous that he might be jumping the gun a bit. But after he got her to step out of the panties, he cast them aside, and then raised himself to a standing position, casually, as if he hadn't been tonguing distance from her heat.

The bastard knew what he'd done, what he'd made her wrongly believe he'd had planned, judging by the amusement in his eyes. Robbing him of time to gloat, she yanked his boxers down and then stood back, staring, as she waited for him to get rid of them.

He seemed in no hurry, and totally unselfconscious of his hard thick arousal aimed heavenward, and her heart pounded so loudly she thought he surely could hear it. When he lowered his gaze, he took his time there, too, leisurely surveying her breasts, her hips, her thighs.

"I've gotta admit, Ms. Whitford..." His gaze came up to rest briefly on her lips and then on her eyes. "You turned out mighty fine."

His approval sent a thrill through her that took her

by surprise. Made her chest tighten with odd and unexpected emotion. Threw her off balance.

She swallowed. "Well, Mr. Conners, I'd have to say the same about you." She'd hoped for something wittier but it was the best she could do.

A hint of a smile danced at the corners of his mouth as he reached for her hand and drew her close. She tilted her head back to meet his kiss. It was gentle yet coaxing and she slid her arms around his waist, enjoying the feel of his erection pressed to her belly. Encouragingly, she wanted to believe that his heart pounded at least as hard as hers and she slid her hands down to mold the firm swell of his buttocks.

He groaned and moved his hips. She pressed harder against him as if he were a magnet and she was a piece of metal helplessly drawn to him.

"Come," he said, his voice hoarse and raspy as he led her to the bed. He yanked the burgundy cover back, and then the matching blanket to expose the white sheets.

He hooked an arm around her waist and took her down with him. Sprawling out in the middle of the bed, he kept hold of her as she lay half on top of him, half off. Laughing, she tried to scramble into a more dignified position, but he flipped her onto her back and pressed her into the mattress with his body.

"Where do you think you're going?" he asked, using the tip of his tongue to trace her jaw.

She arched her neck and he continued his trek

down her throat to her breasts. She sighed. "I'm staying right where I am."

"You're right," he murmured, his warm breath coating her nipple right before he took it into his mouth.

Reflexively she squirmed and he suckled harder as his hand found her other breast. Lightly he pinched the tip between his thumb and forefinger. She moaned with pleasure, and he suckled harder still.

She kneaded the muscles across his back, ran her palms down his taut skin toward his backside but her reach was unsatisfactory. She struggled to gain better access but he wouldn't let her move.

"Jake?"

"Hmm?"

"I have condoms in my purse."

He looked up. "In a hurry, are we?"

"No, I just didn't want to get carried away before we protected ourselves."

"Don't worry. I'm not that carried away." He put his mouth back on her breast, but she couldn't relax.

The remark stung. Of course he probably didn't mean it the way she took it, but he must have sensed her mood change because he lifted his head again and smiled. Without a word, he got up and went to get his jeans. He withdrew a couple of foil packets from the pocket.

Watching the sleek, easy way he moved eased her tension. No question, he not only had the best chest but the best butt she'd ever seen. With or without clothes.

"I'll leave these right here on the nightstand for later," he said, holding up the packets, and then dropping them near the lamp. "Unless you're in a hurry."

She shook her head, unabashedly staring at the tautness and definition of his belly. Even with the interruption, his erection hadn't subsided and it was difficult not to stare there, too. "Did you play sports in high school?"

He nodded, his appreciative gaze slipping down to her breasts. "Why?"

"Which one?"

"Football for three years." He stretched out beside her, and cupped a hand over her breast. "And then hockey for a year in college."

"You went to college?"

Annoyance flashed in his eyes. He released her and lay back with one hand behind his head.

"I'm only surprised because you didn't mention it last night." She curled into him and played with the hair around his navel.

"I dropped out after two years. I hated being in a classroom. Are we just going to talk?"

She ignored the irritation in his voice and tracked the stream of hair down his belly, pleased when he sucked in a breath. He stayed perfectly still while she ran her palm lower. She wrapped her hand around him, and closing his eyes, he groaned.

She continued to explore the length of him, a fascinating combination of smooth satin and the hardness of steel. When she used her finger to probe the tip, he shifted and captured her wrist.

A slow smile lifted his lips as he brought her palm to his mouth. He licked the center, and then kissed it.

She smiled. "Chicken."

"Yeah?" He slid his hand between her thighs.

"Oh." She tried to squeeze her legs together but it was too late. Already she was so wet, one slight graze of his finger was likely to send her rocketing to the ceiling.

"Look who's chicken now." He tongued her earlobe.

"Not chicken, just— Oh, my, God—" She closed her eyes as he drove a finger into her. And then another.

"Relax," he whispered. "I'm not going to hurt you."

"I know. I—" She couldn't think anymore. What was he doing with his fingers? She'd never felt anything like this before...

She threw her head back and he trailed his tongue over the curve of her neck, to her jaw and then nipped at her earlobe. A low whimper escaped her and he covered the sound with his mouth, his lips soft and coaxing, his fingers unrelenting as he probed deeper.

Afraid she'd come too fast, she tried to grasp his forearm, but he wouldn't stop. Unexpectedly he moved to suckle her breasts and she arched off the bed, only intensifying his exploration.

"Jake, we'd better slow down," she murmured.

She felt his smile against her skin, and then his

tongue circled her nipple, slowly, leisurely, heightening her anticipation. He withdrew his fingers but before she could lament the loss, he plunged back inside her. He slid his other hand underneath her bottom and forced an angle to her hips that deepened the penetration.

She jerked when the first wave came, surprising the hell out of her. He used his thumb to rub her clitoris until another shock jerked her again. The spasms increased and she clutched the sheets, tearing them free of the mattress. It was as if her body had received an electrical charge and even as she tried to wiggle away, he stayed with her and the waves kept coming.

Everything got fuzzy. He reached behind and then she thought she heard him fumble with the foil packet. She was still convulsing when he entered her. Filled her with heat and pressure until she didn't think she could take it.

But then he withdrew and used the tip of his silky hard penis to probe the sensitive nub between her folds of flesh. He never once used his hand for guidance, but moved over her, unerringly finding every spot that nearly sent her rocketing once more.

He moaned and she sensed his restraint had begun to slip as he slid in deeper, lowering his body so that his chest grazed her nipples. This time his withdrawal seemed reluctant and when he slid back in he started to pump harder. She tried to meet his thrusts but her body was so spent she couldn't tell if she were moving or not.

He murmured something she didn't understand, and then gave a final thrust before collapsing on her. She couldn't breathe, but not because of his weight. The overwhelming sense of being truly sated was what robbed her of breath. Never had she experienced such physical release.

He rolled off her and, still dazed, she looked at him. He looked pretty wiped out himself. His lids drifted closed, briefly, and then he said, "Hey."

"Hey."

He smiled. "Wow!"

"Yeah." She tried to get up on one elbow but the effort seemed too great.

"You're not leaving yet." It wasn't a question but a simple statement of fact.

"Hadn't even crossed my mind."

"Good." He wound an arm around her and pulled her up against him. She laid her cheek on his chest, his warm, musky skin sedating her, and she closed her eyes.

"Victoria?"

"Hmm?"

"Sleepy?"

She smiled, thinking about how she liked it when *he* called her Victoria. "Not really. What did you have in mind?"

He laughed, his chest vibrating against her cheek. "Give me at least five minutes."

"That's all? At your age? I'm impressed. Ouch!"

"What?"

She brought her head up to meet his hooded eyes. "You know darn well you pinched my butt."

"Sorry. At my age it's hard to remember one moment to the next."

"Okay, we're even." Chuckling, she yawned, and then laid her head back down.

It was really weird being this comfortable with him. Seeing him from a distance for half her life didn't constitute a relationship. Certainly nothing remotely substantial enough to allow for this feeling of familiarity.

Maybe it was just the afterglow from the best sex she'd ever had in her life that made her feel so warm and fuzzy. That idea was a little scary, but kind of nice, too. Maybe it wasn't about familiarity but a simple matter of knowing he wasn't an ax murderer or anything that comforted her.

He ran a hand up her back, and then stroked his way down to her fanny. "Are you snoring?"

"No." She swatted him on the thigh and looked up to see the corners of his mouth twitch.

His humor faded. "You're quiet. Having regrets?"

"No. You?"

"Nope." He shifted his weight, and she pushed up on one elbow to give him room. "Are you going home or staying here tonight?" he asked, glancing at the digital bedside clock.

She got a funny feeling in the pit of her stomach. As great as the sex was, she hoped he didn't think this was going to be an all-night thing. Maybe she should have been more specific regarding her expectations.

"I'll be leaving," she said, taking a look at the clock herself. It was already ten-thirty. "Feel free to stay if you like, though. The room is already paid for."

If she'd expected him to be disappointed, she needn't have worried. He sat up, yawned and stretched, looking totally indifferent. He got to his feet, and mindless of his nudity, went and got his jeans. The sight of him tempted her to call him back to bed.

"I have an early appointment tomorrow." He poked around until he found his boxers, and then looked over at her. "I assumed you didn't want to leave the room together."

She pulled the sheet up to cover herself, and gave a small nod.

He smiled. "Unless you need to go in there," he said, inclining his head toward the bathroom, "I'll only be a couple of minutes."

"Help yourself." She watched him disappear behind the bathroom door, wondering what the hell was wrong with her. He was behaving exactly like she wanted. So why was she the one who was disappointed? Just a little. But still...

Sighing, she started to get up and gather her clothes while she had some privacy. Unlike him, she wasn't quite as comfortable with her body, especially since she'd gained seven pounds during the last two weeks of school and only managed to shed two of them. But what the hell, he'd be gone in the next few minutes and she'd have all the privacy she wanted.

She closed her eyes, thinking about what she'd write to her e-mail buddies. If she were smart, she'd wait a day to tell them about tonight. Wait till she wasn't so tingly and giddy. She didn't want to end up blabbing all the details.

The door opened and she looked up. He was dressed, still tucking in his shirt, the stirrings she felt just watching him alarmed her.

"Okay," he said, meeting her eyes, his totally unreadable. "I'll be shoving off."

She nodded, an inexplicable panic tightening her chest so that she didn't trust herself to speak.

He hesitated, and then headed for the door, and she realized what had her suddenly so tense. What next? Was this it? One night? She hadn't thought things out this far. She hadn't expected to want more. Which was silly. He was awesome. He was...

"Jake?"

He stopped, his hand on the knob, and turned with raised brows.

"Thanks."

He laughed. "Sure."

She wanted to pull the sheet over her face. "I mean, for waiting."

"No problem." He paused, a slight frown on his face. "You parked close, I hope."

"I valet parked."

"Good." He turned the knob.

"Jake, wait." She silently cleared her throat. "I

was wondering—would you be interested in—doing this again?"

He smiled. "You call the shots."

"Tomorrow night?" One more time wouldn't hurt. That hardly constituted a relationship.

"Here?"

"Sure. I won't be late."

He smiled again, and let himself out.

# 5

KAREN SET A FRESH CARAFE of water on the credenza behind Tori's desk. "May I get you anything else, Ms. Whitford?"

"Please call me Tori." She smiled at the secretary she would be sharing with Mallory. Not that her sister showed up at the office more than twice a month.

"Your father likes to keep the office atmosphere formal," Karen said, plucking a dead petal off the bunch of roses Tori had swiped from the garden to put on her desk.

"Okay, then call me Victoria."

The woman didn't even smile.

"That was a joke," Tori muttered. Karen was at least twenty years her senior. It was silly to address Tori as Ms. Whitford. "Whatever makes you comfortable."

Karen started for the door, stopped and turned. "In private I'll call you Tori. In front of your father or the staff it'll be Ms. Whitford."

"Fair enough."

Karen smiled and left, closing the door behind her.

Sighing, Tori sank into her office chair, immediately kicked her shoes off under her desk and bent to massage her left arch. She hadn't worn high heels for years. What the hell had she been thinking?

About Jake mostly.

Not good. There was more to life than sex. He wasn't part of her long-term plan. She shouldn't be thinking about him at all.

She straightened and flexed her foot while she organized the stack of reports Karen had left on her desk. The company's prospectus she'd already reviewed yesterday so she skipped that and went to the profit and loss statements for last quarter.

Just as she started reading, she was interrupted by a brief knock at her door, and then it opened.

"Dad? I thought you were in Dallas."

"I just got back." He entered her office and took a seat across from her. At six-three, he looked too big for the wing chair. Height was one of the many ways Tori took after him. "How's your first day going?"

"Lots of reading."

He looked at the stack she'd been reviewing and frowned. "Hasn't my secretary been sending you this information each quarter?"

"Probably. But I was in school, finishing my master's. I was a little busy."

His frown deepened. "No need to be snide."

"Sorry."

He looked at her for a long silent moment, disapproval lurking in his eyes. "I hope you take more of an interest in this company than your sister has."

"I wouldn't be here if I weren't interested."

A hint of a smile played at the corners of his mouth. "You do have your own mind, I'll give you that."

"Mom's been complaining, huh?"

"She may have mentioned something about your attitude."

Tori sighed. "I think she's trying to marry me off."

He laughed. "Would that be so bad?"

"Have you seen her list of candidates?"

"Don't worry about it. Start getting involved here and you'll be too busy to socialize."

She forced a smile. "True."

Is that what she wanted? She knew working for Whitford Industries wouldn't be easy. Of course she'd be held up to a higher standard. But that didn't bother her. What did, was not knowing if this was what she wanted to do.

"Well, Victoria..." Her father abruptly stood. "I have a lot of work to do. If you need anything, you'll find Karen to be a very competent assistant."

Tori started to make a joke about his political correctness in calling Karen an assistant, but then thought better of it. She just wanted him to go. She wanted him to close the door and for everyone to leave her alone for the afternoon.

"Will I see you at dinner?" she asked his retreating back.

"I doubt it. Tell your mother I have a lot of phone calls to return. No telling what sort of problems will arise."

She nodded absently, even though he hadn't bothered to turn around before leaving. For a few moments, she sat staring at the doorway, wondering if her mother had ever worried that he might be having an affair. His hours were so erratic, and his attention to holidays almost nil.

Probably not. Work was his mistress. God, what a life. Is that what she had to look forward to? No, not her. She wouldn't go there. She could balance career and a social life...maybe even a family at some point...

She turned her attention back to the reports but her concentration was gone. Her thoughts kept straying to Jake, to the women at the center, to her friend Kathryn at school...

Not bothering to put on her heels, she got up and closed the door, and then got her laptop out of her briefcase. She'd waited long enough to report on last night. She wouldn't settle down until she got it out of her system.

To: The Gang at Eve's Apple
From: Angel@EvesApple.com
Subject: Bliss!!!
You advised me to be direct so any cracks about me moving fast will be swiftly dealt with. <G> Last night I met J at a hotel. And although I don't wanna kiss and tell—Holy shit!!! I have no words to describe the mind-blowing sex we had. He was incredible! More than my feeble brain could imagine.

If anything, after all those years of lusting after the guy, I thought the experience would have fallen short of my expectations. Sheesh, was I wrong. The trouble is, one night hardly got it out of my system. I want more!!! In fact, we have plans to meet again tonight. The thought is making concentration really hard. I'm trying to work—it's my first day in the office, but I can't seem to focus.

Have I told you what a great body he has!?! I mean, I'd seen him without a shirt lots of times, but last night, without a thread to distract me, oh, my, God... I better quit writing this damn e-mail.

I have something else I want to bounce off you guys. Not about J. It has to do with my mother and coming home again and that sort of

Tori stopped typing when her cell phone rang. She looked at the caller ID before answering. All thoughts of e-mails and Jake faded. It was the center. They very rarely called her.

She answered the call, and at the same time sent her e-mail and then signed off.

"OKAY, POP." Jake closed the ancient red truck's creaking tailgate. "Get back inside. You don't need to supervise me."

"Did you load the small pruning sheers? The Princess Daisy roses are fragile, son. You know the ones I'm talking about—those salmon-colored ones by the gazebo." He stood at the edge of the porch, leaning heavily on his cane. He looked old, his face weathered from years of too much sun. Hard to believe he was only sixty-three.

"I know, Pop."

"And don't forget the Scarlett O'Haras. They like—"

"Enough, Pop. I know. Now get inside and put your feet up, or I'll park this old lemon and take the keys so you don't get any crazy ideas."

Muttering, he waved a disgusted hand, and turned to hobble into the house.

Shaking his head, Jake opened the driver's door and climbed inside. He felt like a kid again. Sneaking around, misleading his father. Hector was perfectly capable of taking care of the Whitfords' gardens. The guy had worked for Jake for six years. Longer than any of his other employees. Other than letting himself get distracted by a pair of breasts now and then, Hector was reliable and knew almost as much about landscaping as Jake did.

Still, it was easier for Jake to let his father think he was personally taking care of the Whitfords. Even though he had to act like a sixteen-year-old, pretending to pick up the old red truck and then handing it off to Hector at the end of the driveway.

It wasn't just about not wanting to see Victoria. Hell, he doubted she'd come traipsing down with any more lemonade. It wasn't about not wanting to get his hands dirty, either. In fact, it had been kind of interesting to get close to the earth again. He'd spent too much time at a desk the past two years. It was good to get out in the fresh air for a change. The added bonus, he had to admit, was Victoria.

The whole experience seemed surreal. After her being forbidden fruit for all those years. He'd gotten halfway down the driveway and glanced in his rearview mirror. No sign of his father. The poor old guy would have heart failure if he knew where Jake had been last night. Where he was going to be...he looked at his watch. In ten hours. Shit, he shouldn't be so anxious. But what the hell...that was arguably the best sex he'd ever had.

Just thinking about her long, smooth legs got his heart pumping. She had to be about five-eight, maybe taller. Hard to tell when she wore those high heels. He was just barely six feet himself and with heels on, she nearly met him eye to eye.

But beyond the distracting thoughts of Victoria, the real problem was his full calendar. He had a prospective client to meet at eleven, and a meeting with a Forever Green representative at three-thirty. He dreaded that appointment, even though his lawyer would do most of the talking. Jake would sit there, nod, smile, and then take the money and run.

JAKE LOOKED UP from the room service menu when he heard a knock and then a key in the door.

Victoria opened it, still in work clothes, a navy-blue suit and white shirt, dark-colored hose and ridiculously high heels. Except that they made her legs look so good that he had to look away or embarrass himself. "What time did you get here?"

"About fifteen minutes ago."

"Gee, I thought I was early and then I got to the front desk and found out you'd already checked in."

He shrugged. "I was already in the area and it seemed foolish to go home first."

Her gaze lowered to his striped blue-and-white shirt, khakis and brown loafers. Which were pretty much his work clothes when he had to attend meetings. He expected her to ask why he wasn't wearing jeans but instead she pulled her purse strap off her shoulder and dug around inside.

He went back to perusing the room service menu, trying not to think about how those legs were going to feel wrapped around his waist. "Are you hungry?"

"What?" She looked up. "I hadn't really thought about it yet."

He snorted. "I've been thinking about it since lunch. I figured I'd order a few appetizers and a bottle of wine. Any preference?"

"Anything but rose." She pulled out some cash. "Here."

"What's that?"

"For the room." She dropped the money on the table beside him, and then kicked off her shoes in the corner by the desk. "I hope that's enough. I'd planned on using a credit card so that's all I have."

He stayed silent, trying like hell to hold on to his temper. Finally, when he trusted himself enough to speak, he said, "You paid for the room last night. It's my turn."

"Yeah, but I'm the one who— Look, this place is expensive. I don't expect you to fork out—" She stopped and moistened her lips. "You're angry."

"Damn right."

"Why?"

"Put your fancy Ivy League education to the test. Think about it."

She lifted her chin, her eyes sparkling with temper. "Is that resentment I hear?"

"Maybe, but not because of what you think."

"Please, by all means." She gestured an invitation with her hand. "Tell me what I'm thinking."

Jake put the menu aside, his appetite shot to hell. Her sarcasm was the last straw. "I don't resent the fact that your family could afford a top-notch education. Good for you. Everyone should have that privilege. But I do resent you treating me like a toy poodle."

Her eyes widened. "What?"

He waited for realization to register in her face. Nothing happened. He laughed humorlessly. "You don't even get it."

"No, I don't." She folded her arms across her chest, her eyes wary. "I told you exactly what I wanted from you and you agreed. I don't see the toy poodle connection."

Okay, she'd been honest, he'd give her that much. He shook his head. He knew he was being touchy because she'd assumed he couldn't afford the room.

"Yeah, I agreed, but that doesn't mean I don't want to be treated like an equal."

"Is this all because I wanted to pay for the room? Because that's pretty damn sexist of you."

He started to ask how that made him sexist since she paid for it last night, but reconsidered. They'd both gotten too hot under the collar to bring this to a conclusion. He was hungry, and still a little ticked that the meeting with Forever Green hadn't gone like he'd planned.

He hated all the deadlines being shoved down his throat. He hated corporate bullshit. Sometimes he thought his father had the right idea. Work for someone else. Let them have the headaches.

"Look." He got to his feet. "Let's do this some other time."

She blinked, reared her head back slightly. "This isn't that big a deal."

He bent down to fist the bills she'd left on the table. "Don't forget this," he said, and forced them into her hands, brushing against her breasts in the process. He'd probably kick himself later.

Her expression indicated she didn't want to take it, but she reluctantly gave in. Regret darkened her hazel eyes. She gave him a weak smile. "You want to order something from room service before you go? We probably both could use a glass of wine."

He kept on course to the door, but then stopped. She did look pretty miserable. Not his problem. "I'll

pick something up on the way home. Take care,
Victoria."


To: The Gang at Eve's Apple
From: Angel@EvesApple.com
Subject: Aaargh!!!
The guy's a jerk. We were supposed to meet tonight, which we did, but then he blew it. Accused
me of treating him like a toy poodle. Got all mad
and indignant just because I wanted to reimburse
him for the hotel room, which he paid for because
he got there first. Never would have figured him
for a chauvinist. Damn! I know I'm rambling but
I'm pissed. Or can't you tell?
     Any of you out there? I really need a shoulder
tonight. Or a punching bag.
Love,
Angel, who's thinking about getting good and
sloshed


She quickly sent off the e-mail, hoping Taylor or
Kelly or one of the Barbaras happened to be on line.
They all tended to pick up their mail in the evenings.
She checked her watch. Only eight-fifteen. She
should have been writhing in ecstasy about now.
Not sitting on her bed, alone, with her laptop, and
drinking a glass of strawberry Kool-Aid, enjoying
every last gram of sugar.
     Sighing, she set the laptop aside and went to her
closet for a nightshirt. After selecting the one with

Mickey Mouse on the front, she slipped out of her robe and pulled the shirt over her head.

God, she was going to miss her walk-in closet when she moved to an apartment. Of course some of the newer ones had great bathrooms with sunken tubs and giant closets. But would she be able to afford one of those? Hell, she hadn't even asked about her salary. Some businesswoman.

It wouldn't matter, anyway. She'd find something suitable, probably not unlike the place she'd lived in while in school. Freedom and independence was the tradeoff. She wouldn't have to sneak off to hotels. She could have Jake over anytime she wanted...

She stopped in her tracks. Jake was not going to be popping over, nor would she be inviting him to do so. The only thing they had in common was sex. And she might have screwed that up, too.

She got back in bed and piled up all three pillows behind her, wishing like crazy she felt she could talk to Mallory. But even though they'd more or less kept in touch over the last seven years, Tori felt distanced from her. Which really smarted since they hadn't even started getting close until a year before Tori left for college.

Mallory would be the only person who'd understand Tori's misgivings about her career. Not misgivings, really. She was happy to be included in such a successful, thriving business. But all their lives it was assumed they'd enter the family business. No one ever asked what their major would be in college. No question. An MBA it was. When it came time for marriage, there'd be no leeway there, either. Rich and influential was the core criteria.

After surfing through the Neiman Marcus Web site and checking out the new fall fashions, she went back to e-mail and found that Babs had written back.

To: Angel
From: BarbaraJ@EvesApple.com
Subject: I feel your pain
Angel! How awful! I wish I could give you a big hug. I know how excited you were. About the toy poodle thing—sounds like his pride's hurt. Maybe he would have preferred stud muffin? :) Sorry, I had to throw that in.

You were up-front with him. You did nothing wrong. Screw him. At least you had that one night. I do have a question, though. Why a hotel? Who's idea was that?

Good grief, girlfriend, I hope he isn't married.

Anyway, take care, good luck, and don't get sloshed. The headache won't be worth it.
Love,
Babs

Like that was helpful. Tori sighed and got out of the e-mail to check the other two messages that had popped up. Taylor had also written, bless her. She'd have something worthwhile to say.

To: Angel
From: Taylor@EvesApple.com
Subject: Trouble in paradise

Ah, sweetie, I'm so sorry. Maybe tomorrow after you've both cooled off you'll be able to talk. It doesn't matter if this was a one-time deal. I'm sure you don't want to leave things like this.

Gotta tell you, though, sounds like there's more to it than you spilled. You said you didn't really know him, right? So it's not like you guys have baggage or past issues... Sorry, but I don't get it. You were honest, explained what you wanted from him. Doesn't sound like it was your fault. Either he had a bad day or you triggered some old pride issue. I don't know...

What's up with going to a hotel? Could that be part of the problem? Wish I could help. Write soon.

Love,
Taylor

Tori groaned. What was the big deal about going to a hotel? She closed her laptop. Of course her friends didn't realize she lived with her parents, that she couldn't very well twist Jake's arm to offer up his place. Not that she would have accepted. A hotel was neutral, anonymous, away from nosy family and friends. There was nothing at all wrong with meeting there. She couldn't think of a better place in the world to have meaningless sex.

# 6

FROM HER BEDROOM WINDOW, Tori saw him near the pool, inspecting the leaves of her mother's prize roses, the ones that had been featured in some magazine last year. Jake had been standing there a while, peering in for close looks, a frown on his face, obviously concerned about something. Maybe now wasn't a good time to pretend to be strolling in the gardens and that she just happened to come across him.

Tough. She was going crazy, distracted as hell, and she knew damn well the insanity wasn't going to end until she talked with him.

The ground looked a little muddy from last night's brief rain and she slipped on some rubber flip-flops before heading downstairs. She heard Isabelle upstairs, cleaning one of the bathrooms, and was pretty sure her mother was on the phone in the study.

Mallory undoubtedly was moping in her room. With Richard away on business for three weeks, and the renovation of their house still two months away from completion, she didn't do much but stick to her room and read or watch television. And probably drink too much.

Tori hated butting into Mallory's affairs, but she wasn't going to be able to keep her mouth shut much longer. It broke her heart to see her beautiful, once spirited sister withering away. If Tori ended up upsetting her and distancing her further, it was a risk she was willing to take.

The temperature was horrible, the air heavy with humidity, one thing she hadn't missed about Houston while she was away. Of course the condition was excellent for growing healthy plants, brilliant colored flowers. Not having the garden to look at every day would definitely be the worst thing about living in an apartment.

She was still quite a distance away when Jake looked up, almost as if he'd sensed her coming. Inexplicably she felt self-conscious all of a sudden, and wished he'd go back to inspecting the roses. But he kept his focus on her, even when she slid on the soft damp ground and nearly ended up on her butt. Fortunately she righted herself before getting up close and personal with the oleander bushes.

"You okay?" he asked.

"Yeah. Mea culpa. I should have stayed on the path." She sighed. "But following rules haven't been my long suit lately. Anyway, I just wanted to tell you how great everything looks. These roses are worthy of a magazine cover."

He smiled, making no effort to conceal his interest in the brevity of her shorts. "Is that really why you came out here, Victoria?"

She hesitated. "Well, no, I went swimming yesterday and I think I forgot my—" The challenge in his eyes canceled her need to lie or play coy. "I came out to see you, and judging by the way you've been staring at me, you're pretty damn glad I did."

"Touché." He pulled a rag out of his back pocket and wiped his forehead and the back of his neck, his rounded bicep straining against his T-shirt sleeve. "So where's the lemonade?"

"Oh. I was about to get ready for work. I didn't think of it."

"Fine. You already got me in the sack so you don't think you have to woo me anymore."

She started to laugh, and then quickly glanced over her shoulder. "Would you be quiet?"

"Nobody's around." His gaze went toward the second story. "Of course someone could be watching from a window. Doesn't that concern you?"

Reflexively she started to turn around and check, but caught herself. "Why should it?"

"I doubt you want to be seen with me."

"That's ridiculous." She sighed, reflecting on the girls' e-mails. They thought she'd hurt his pride. Maybe they were right. "Here's the thing. I don't give a damn about who sees us together. But my mother thinks she has my life planned and she can be a real pain in the ass if it looks as though I wavered off her course. I don't need her bombarding me with a hundred questions about you."

"I'm curious." Amusement danced at the corners of his mouth. "What sort of questions would she ask about me?"

She glanced at her watch. "Are we going to talk about my mother, or make plans to see each other again?"

"Let's see..." He pursed his lips, and looked off toward the pool.

"Very funny, but if I were you I wouldn't quit your day job."

He gave her a lopsided smile that made her tummy flutter. "Tonight?"

"Okay— Oh, shoot. I can't. I have this dinner my mom set up. How about tomorrow?"

He nodded. "Same place?"

She thought for a moment. "You choose this time."

Suspicion narrowed his eyes. "Why?"

She shrugged. "I haven't been around for a while. You probably know someplace better."

"I don't usually meet women in hotels."

God, the temptation to ask if he used his back seat was almost too much to resist but she didn't want to get in a conversation where he'd ask her to go to his place. She'd have to say no, and then there'd be questions or assumptions and, damn, this was supposed to be easy. This was just about sex for goodness' sakes.

"Okay," she said slowly, "then help me think of a place that's closer and cheaper."

His expression darkened.

"Even if we were to split the cost," she quickly added, figuring it was that stupid ego thing again, "that place is pricey."

"Fine."

But it wasn't. She could tell by the tightening of his jaw. "Look, it was okay for one night," she said. "I didn't know we were going to be—well, you know—"

That made him relax, his mouth twitching. "What?"

"Screw you. You know what I'm saying." She tried not to smile. "Anyway, I'm looking for an apartment and I—"

He looked surprised. "You are?"

"Yeah. I thought I mentioned it."

"Maybe." He shrugged. "Where are you looking?"

"I haven't started yet. I figured I'd do that this weekend. Anyway, I've gotta go." She glanced over her shoulder toward the house. "Mind if I swipe a few roses for my desk?"

"Hey, they're your flowers."

"No, they're my mothers, as she often reminds us, and if she knew I was picking them she'd have a friggin' fit."

He gave her a wry smile. "I promise not to tell."

"What about those?" She pointed to the lavender ones. "They look fragile and I have a stop to make. Think they'll last okay?"

He frowned and looked at her like she was nuts. "How would I know?"

"Well, you know more about flowers than I do."

"I doubt it."

"But that's your job."

His mouth curved in an enigmatic smile. "You've been away a long time, Victoria. Don't think you know everything about me."

"YOU'VE REACHED Safe Haven Women's Center. How can I help you?" Tori waited patiently for the caller to respond. It wasn't unusual for the women calling to be reluctant to ask for help. Most of them had been physically and emotionally abused and picking up the phone was a huge step. "Hello? This is Safe Haven—"

"Bitch! Leave my wife alone." The man slammed down the phone.

Sighing, Tori replaced the receiver. And then there were husbands whose wives had stayed at Safe Haven for a while, before returning home to assert their new independence. Their husbands would sometimes call to curse and threaten. Generally Tori ignored them and hung up. But sometimes she let her temper get the better of her and made a few choice comments about the guy's manhood.

Kathryn, the center's director, had reminded Tori on several occasions not to get emotionally involved and to watch her heated responses, but it made Tori so damn angry to see these women go back into such horrible situations. She wanted to shake them into realizing they didn't have to be scared, that there were people who'd help them for as long as it took.

The counselors repeatedly warned the women about returning, that their husbands needed professional help first, but invariably the bastards would call and sweet-talk their wives into going home, making the same promises they'd never been able to keep. And in a couple of weeks Tori would see the women, often with a blackened eye or broken arm, but only if the center had enough beds when they called. Those were the lucky ones.

"Hey."

Tori glanced over her shoulder at Kathryn who'd just entered the office. "Hey."

"Any more calls?"

"Just an irate husband."

"Good. We have only one bed left." Kathryn looked tired. She pulled the elastic band from her blond ponytail and rearranged her hair before tying it up again, and then grabbed the clipboard they kept next to the hot line phone and made a note of the bed she'd just given away.

"It's been quiet all afternoon," Tori said, wishing it weren't so because it gave her way too much time to think about Jake and his cryptic remark.

"Yeah? Just wait until tomorrow. Full moon."

Tori rolled her eyes. "That's right." It always got crazy busy on full moon nights. "Look, why don't you go grab some sleep? I'll be here for another hour."

She shook her head. "Thanks, but I have a ton of stuff to do for the fund-raiser. The board wants everything yesterday."

"Tough. It's not as if you don't have a center to run."

Kathryn smiled patiently. "Fund-raisers keep the center in existence."

"Yeah, I know." Tori couldn't think of a person she admired more than Kathryn. Always patient and sensible. Tireless in her efforts to champion battered women. "What can I do to help?"

"You're doing it." She picked up a stack of envelopes and flyers. "Man the phone until Crystal gets here."

"All I'm doing is filing and addressing envelopes while I wait for the phone to ring. Isn't there something else I can do?"

Kathryn hesitated. "You work all day and then come here in the afternoon and evenings. You do so much already—"

"Look who's talking." Tori snorted. "I don't think you ever go home."

"It's my job."

"To kill yourself?"

Kathryn sighed heavily and rubbed the back of her neck. "I'll be in my office."

"I apologize. I didn't mean to push or butt in."

"I know." She smiled. "This isn't like a corporate job, Tori. You can't just pack whatever you didn't get done for the day into a briefcase and take it home. But you'll get no complaints from me. I knew what I signed up for. I'm right where I want to be."

Tori sat there, overcome with an emotion she didn't understand. Not sadness, exactly. Wistful?

"Look, as humbling as it is to admit it, I have a secretary with not a whole lot to do at the moment. Isn't there something she can do as far as flyers or programs or mailings?"

Interest lit Kathryn's eyes. "Would she mind?"

"Not Karen. I know she'd love to help. In fact, she'd just like to have something to do besides look busy."

"What about your boss?"

"My dad?" Tori made a face. "Maybe he'll do me a favor and fire me."

Kathryn laughed. "If you're sure..."

"Bring it on."

Tori spent the next hour with Kathryn, going over her to-do list, consisting of calls to be made, thank-yous to be written and sent, reports to type, invoices to reconcile. It was amazing she got anything done. Yet she was totally organized, and incredibly focused.

Tori envied her. She envied her passion, her determination. Kathryn was exactly who Tori wanted to be when she grew up. Maybe she'd get lucky and her father really would fire her. Oh, God. She couldn't afford to go there. So she wouldn't.

JAKE PULLED INTO THE HOTEL'S parking lot right behind Tori. He spotted her sporty car right away. She didn't see him, so he parked his SUV in the first vacant spot the next row over and doubled back to meet her. She probably wouldn't like it. She'd want them to go in separately. Fine. She could tell him point-blank. Spell it out that she was embarrassed to be seen with him.

Again, she wore work clothes, but this time without the suit jacket, and he stared at the perfect curve of her backside as she bent to retrieve something from the passenger side, and then at the two huge sacks she pulled out. "Jeez, you staying for the week?"

She turned around, laughing. "Good, you're just in time to help me. Here."

He took the bag she handed him. "Give me the other one, too."

"I've got it." She closed the door with her hip and pressed the remote lock, her gaze leveled on him. "Better hold that one from underneath. It's heavy and I don't—"

Jake frowned. She was staring. "What? I have spinach in my teeth?"

"Huh?" She blinked, and her cheeks got pink. "Sorry."

"What's wrong?"

"Nothing. Really." She looked away and adjusted her purse strap. "You look nice."

"Oh. Thanks," he mumbled. Hell, all he'd done was gotten a haircut. He'd shaved again, too. No big deal. He switched his attention to the bag. "What's in here?"

She cleared her throat. "Some wine and munchies. In case you haven't had dinner."

He'd chosen the hotel because it was closer. "I know it's not the Ritz but I'm sure they have room service," he said, his defenses starting to rise.

"Yeah, but thirty bucks for a bottle of wine and

twelve for a small bowl of chips? I don't think so." She slid him a sheepish look. "If I want to get a decent apartment I'll have to stick to a budget."

That surprised him, both her seriousness about getting an apartment and her need to follow a budget. "Thanks. I *am* kind of hungry."

"Good. I—"

He took the bag out of her hands, set them both on the hood of her car, and then slid his arms around her waist and hauled her up against him. She didn't look around, just gazed up at him, her eyes sparkling with excitement. He lowered his head and she eagerly met his lips.

He kissed her gently at first, and then hard and she immediately parted her lips, receiving his tongue with fevered enthusiasm. Ironically he was the one who withdrew first when someone laughingly yelled from a passing car to get a room.

"We should go inside," he whispered, and took a nip at her lower lip.

She tilted her head back but looked as if she could barely lift her lids. "Uh-huh."

"Someone has to check in." He stroked her hair, so soft, each strand baby-fine, yet thick and shiny.

"I'll do it. It's my turn to pay."

"You brought dinner. I'll get the room tab."

"No, it's—"

He slid a hand down to the small of her back and pulled her closer so she could feel his arousal. "Do you want to stand out here and argue, or go in and get naked?"

Her lips curved and she looked at him through slits. "You don't play fair."

"So?"

Laughing softly, she pushed away and turned to lead him between her car and a Lincoln. He smiled and grabbed the bags she'd obviously forgotten. To his amazement, she headed straight for the lobby. When they got there, she stood off to the side while he checked in but that she was even in the vicinity was something.

Neither of them spoke on the way to the elevator, and when an older man got in the car with them, they stayed silent. Lots of eye contact, though. Teasing looks that excited him as if she'd drawn her nails down his back.

He didn't let her get away with it. Strategically moving his hips, he gave her a start, and she retaliated by pinching his butt. They finally got to their floor, and she preceded him out of the car with a remarkably straight face.

"You're lucky I took pity on you," he said, handing her a bag so he could insert the key into the lock.

"How so?"

"I thought about embarrassing the hell out of you in that elevator." He opened the door and waited for her to go in first.

"Ha. How?"

He set the bag he carried on the floor and kicked the door closed with his boot. Fear and excitement shined in her face and she started to dart away but he caught her by the wrist and made her lower her bag to the floor.

"What are you doing?" she asked in a breathless whisper.

He slid a hand under her skirt and smiled. "Searching for treasure."

She laughed, a kind of cute girlie giggle that pleased him. "Impatient little devil, aren't you?"

He reached the top of her hose at midthigh, held up by a garter belt. "Nice. I didn't think women wore these anymore."

"They don't. Makes it too easy for guys like you."

He chuckled. "Guys like me, huh? What's that supposed to mean?"

Her lips started to curve in one of those smug smiles she sometimes gave him, but he moved his hand higher, his fingers violating the elastic of her panties, and she jerked.

"You were saying?"

"Okay." Challenge gleamed in her eyes and she reached between them, targeting his arousal.

"Ah, you got me. I give up." He probed with his fingers until she started moving her hips.

She moaned, and then retreated. "Jake. Wait."

"What's wrong?"

"I want to take a shower. I've been at work all day and then I went—I had someplace else to go."

"Can I take one with you?" He kissed the side of her neck, surprised when she hesitated. After letting the silence stretch a moment, he removed his hand and pulled back to look at her.

"It'll be faster if I take one by myself."

"You in a hurry?"

She lifted a shoulder, her eyes not quite meeting his. "No. I thought maybe you could open the wine and set out the cheese and crackers so we can eat when I'm done."

"Okay." He stepped back to retrieve the bags. Something was obviously bothering her. He knew she couldn't be embarrassed about her body. He'd covered most of it with either his hands or tongue. But he'd give her the space she wanted. No problem. That didn't stop his curiosity, though.

"Jake?"

He grabbed a bag in each hand and straightened.

She'd already started to unbutton her blouse, exposing the tops of her pink lace bra and two mounds of creamy flesh. "Thanks."

"For what?" He forced his gaze to her face. Hard enough to concentrate but when she got to the last button he was a goner. "Never mind," he said, walking away. "But I'd suggest you get your sweet little fanny in that bathroom before I make you forget that shower."

"Promises, promises." She laughed, a soft taunting sound that had him dropping the bags and turning on her with a growl. She gasped and scampered off to the bathroom, closing the door behind her.

He smiled when he heard the click of the lock.

# 7

TORI TURNED OFF the steamy water. Great for her pores but horrible for her hair. She tried not to get her hair wet, but that didn't matter. Any sleekness she'd managed to create with her round brush and blow-dryer was long gone. So was most of her makeup.

She thought about dashing out to grab her purse and then reapplying the more important touches like blush and mascara, but she doubted Jake would notice. And she shouldn't care if he did. She was a willing partner. That was his only concern. It wasn't as if this was a date.

In fact, that's why she'd shied away from the whole shower thing. Too intimate. Just like breakfast in bed, or doing the Sunday crossword together. Maybe he thought that because she'd brought dinner the game was changing.

No, that was silly. She rubbed herself dry and liberally applied some lotion provided by the hotel. The steam obscured most of the mirror and she had to clear a spot in order to assess the damage. Her nose was a little red but she still had some mascara on.

Luckily she'd been blessed with smooth, clear skin that required only a tinted moisturizer so she was okay in that department.

She glanced disdainfully at her discarded skirt and blouse and decided a towel would be enough for now. Thinking about the look on Jake's face when he suggested she get in the bathroom, her nerve endings tingled with excitement. She doubted she'd be wearing even the towel for long. But she carefully wrapped the dry one around her, pushed her fingers through her hair, hoping it looked artfully tousled and not just a mess.

As soon as she stepped into the room and Jake looked up from the wine he was pouring, she realized he wasn't going to notice her hair. His gaze started at her breasts and leisurely ran down to where the towel ended midthigh.

"Nice wine," he said, returning his attention to the bottle of merlot. "Very nice." One side of his mouth went up. "That's some budget you have."

"Hey, I'm not that dense. I swiped it from my dad's wine cellar."

He laughed, a really great laugh that came from deep down, husky and warm and entirely too endearing.

She cleared her throat. "I'll have you know I stuck to one hell of a budget while I was away at school."

Amusement lit his eyes. "Your parents put you on a budget?"

"No, I put myself on one. My spending money

came from a trust fund my grandmother left me and I didn't want to blow the whole thing in six years."

He had a funny look on his face she couldn't interpret. Probably had to do with her having a trust fund. She wasn't going to apologize for it. At least she didn't take for granted the privilege and opportunity the money afforded her.

"Let's eat before we get started," he said, and poured a second glass of wine in the plastic champagne glass she'd brought.

She flinched at his choice of words. It sounded as if he was talking about work. So cold and impersonal. Which is what she wanted, she reminded herself. "Good, I'm hungry," she said, careful to avoid his eyes, not wanting him to read anything in hers.

He'd set the crackers and cheese on the desklike table near the window, and she busied herself with making a selection. She took a small wedge of Camembert and another of Gouda, and then dug through the bag, looking for the red grapes.

"Here." He held up the bunch, and then waited for her to walk to him.

"I'll trade you a piece of Camembert."

He smiled and plucked one of the grapes from the bunch. "I can get my own cheese. I had something else in mind."

"Oh?" Her heart pounded. "What?"

"Open."

She tilted her head back but kept her gaze on him

as he lowered the grape into her mouth. "Mmm, nice and juicy."

"Just what I was thinking." His gaze lingered on her breasts before reaching her eyes.

She chuckled. "You're awful."

"Think so?" He grabbed the end of her towel.

"Hey."

"What?"

She couldn't back up or she'd lose the towel altogether. "I thought we were going to eat first."

"Eat," he ordered, and then yanked the towel off.

Tori gasped and nearly dropped her food. "Not fair."

"Interesting how you have this delusion that I mean to play fair."

She tried unsuccessfully to grab the towel. Standing there, exposed, made her feel too vulnerable. Awkward as hell. "Please give me the towel back."

His lips curved in a wicked smile, his gaze taking her in. "Come and get it."

She stepped forward and made a swipe for the towel, but he jerked it out of reach. "Hey."

"You have to be faster than that."

She stood perfectly still, trying to give the appearance of defeat, and then grabbed for it again.

He was too quick.

"Fine. I'll go put on my clothes." She turned to go to the bathroom but laughing, he captured her hand and drew her back.

"Okay, here."

She took the towel and wrapped it around herself.

Before she could tuck in the front, he cupped both breasts, swiftly kissing each and then sighed. "I'm going to miss these babies."

She had to laugh as she secured the front of the towel. His forlorn expression was enough to tickle her. "I thought we were supposed to be eating."

Interest piqued in his face and he opened his mouth, but then promptly shut it again.

"Don't say it."

"I'm not." He grabbed a couple of crackers and broke off a hunk of Gouda. "This is my favorite cheese."

"Mine, too."

"Why don't you take off your towel?"

She grinned, shaking her head. "You have a one-track mind."

"No, two tracks. They just both go to the same station."

"Tell you what. Why don't *you* take *your* clothes off?"

He shrugged. "Okay." And then immediately pulled up the hem of his T-shirt, and pulled it off, revealing his flat stomach and smattering of hair across his chest. "See, I'm easy."

"Yes, you are."

He grinned and unbuckled his belt, unsnapped his jeans. But then he paused to take a sip of wine and bite into the cheese. "Better warn you. Gouda makes me horny."

"Right. Like you need help."

"True." He took another sip of wine and then sat

on the edge of the bed to take off his boots. "Will you take the towel off now?"

She nibbled on a cracker. "You didn't say please."

"Please."

"No."

His look of disbelief made her smile. "That's not—" He stopped.

"Fair?"

"Eat your cheese and crackers." With a grumpy expression that made her giggle, he slid the jeans down his legs, and then kicked them off, leaving him in a pair of silky brown boxer shorts.

His calves were muscular as if he worked on them, and then she remembered that he'd played football and ran track. Maybe that's what made them look so perfect, as if they had been designed and sculpted. That and good genes.

She hadn't been so lucky in the gene department. She and Mallory had both inherited saddlebags from their mother. No amount of diet and exercise had managed to eliminate the small bulges on Tori's outer thighs. Even working with a personal trainer hadn't much helped Mallory nor their mother. Some legacy.

She took another nibble of cheese and winced at the thought of how much fat was in one crummy bite. Jake obviously wasn't worried. Not that he had to be. She watched him enjoy another hunk of cheese, and pour a second glass of wine.

"Ready?" he asked, holding the bottle up to her.

"Sure." She moved closer and held out her glass.

He poured, set down the bottle and then surprised her by taking her glass. Before she knew it, he yanked off the towel again.

"Damn it."

He smiled, and slid his arms around her, pulling her close. With him still sitting on the bed, his face met her breasts and he took full advantage, suckling one, and then the other. She wound her arms around his neck and he buried his face against her, moaning, his hands running down over her buttocks.

"You feel so good," he whispered. "So soft, so silky."

She closed her eyes, enjoying the vibration of his words against her skin. He tightened his hold, his palm pressing into her backside, and he ran his tongue around each nipple until her flesh prickled with anticipation.

Her knees grew weak and she clutched his shoulders trying to steady herself. His hands slid from her backside to the back of her thighs and he drew her impossibly closer. Engrossed in the enjoyment of his talented mouth, she hadn't realized he'd moved one hand between them until he slipped it between her thighs.

She sucked in a breath as he found the wetness that had pooled there, the slick heat making her struggle to stay on her feet. He inserted a finger and she moved her hips forward as he drove deeper.

"I want to taste you," he whispered.

She opened her eyes, feeling a little dazed, seeing that his eyes were glassy, too.

"Lie down with me." He coaxed with his finger, with his mouth on her breast.

She went boneless, and when he withdrew his finger to maneuver her onto the bed, she allowed him complete control. He lay back and tugged her into place beside him, his hands continuing to rove her body as if he couldn't get enough of her. That heady idea alone excited her beyond belief and she eagerly reached into the elastic of his boxers to find him hard and ready.

He groaned with pleasure and yanked off the underwear. She tried to reach for him again but he rose to a kneeling position and spread her thighs.

Her first instinct was to use the sheet to cover herself, but the heat in his gaze drove away any insecurities. He stared down at her for a moment and then his gaze rose to hers. The intensity in his eyes should have sent her running, but she held her breath as he lowered his mouth and then used his tongue to give her the most explosive orgasm she'd ever had.

A KNOCK AT HER OPEN office door made Tori look up.

Karen poked her head in. "I'm going to lunch. You've been so hard at work all morning I figured you didn't realize what time it was. Can I bring you back a sandwich or something?"

Tori smiled, shook her head and tried not to look guilty. Yeah, she'd been really hard at work, all right. Staring at the same report for the past two hours and thinking about last night. About Jake. "Thanks, anyway. I'd like to get out of the office for a while.

"I don't blame you." Karen glanced at her watch. "Well, I gotta go. I'm meeting Cindy from contracts in the lobby."

Tori watched her go, and then threw down her pen. Strictly a prop. She hadn't made a single notation or digested a scrap of information about their overseas factories in Hong Kong or Taiwan.

True, her thoughts kept drifting back to Jake and the three incredible hours they'd spent last night. Today, muscles were hurting that she hadn't even known she had. But that wasn't the only thing distracting her from the report. It was plain old boring. A mess of numbers and statistics and forecasts she didn't give a damn about. Of course they were important and she had to learn the guts of the company but she missed dealing with people.

And damn it, she missed Jake.

Which was incredibly foolish. Stupid, really. Not only had it been only thirteen hours since she'd seen him but it was only about sex. She certainly couldn't have that twenty-four/seven.

Could she?

She closed her eyes and pinched the bridge of her nose, uncomfortable with the idea that maybe this was about a little more than sex. She truly enjoyed his company. He was witty and relaxed, unlike the stuffed shirts who worked for her father. Of course Jake's job was done once he left the garden.

Oh, God, was she going to end up like all the other executives in the company, living for work, spending hours in the office after sane people had left for the day.

She looked at her watch wondering what Jake was doing right now. Had he stopped for lunch? Without rush hour traffic, she could be home in twenty minutes.

That was crazy.

Of course they hadn't discussed another night to meet.

That would be reason enough to make an attempt to see him. Assuming he planned on seeing her again.

The sudden thought unnerved her. What if he hadn't brought it up because he had no intention of seeing her again? If not, she shouldn't care. It had been fun while it lasted.

The hell with it. She stuck the stack of papers in her desk, locked it and then grabbed her purse. She was hungry. Even if he weren't there, no big deal. She wanted lunch. No big deal at all.

HE WASN'T THERE. The old red truck was parked in the back but she could only see the other guy, Hector. She'd left her car in the circular driveway and had gotten a good view of the front gardens and Jake wasn't there, either. It was still possible they'd split up so she craned her neck at the kitchen window to see the area by the pond.

"He didn't come today. Just the Mexican guy." Mallory had entered the kitchen, a drink in her hand. "Who isn't too bad himself," she added as she stopped beside Tori and stared out the window.

Tori wrinkled her nose at the smell of gin. "I didn't know you were here."

"Oh, hell, I'm always here. Where else would I be?"

"At the office?"

Mallory snorted. "Gee, that sounds like fun. Why didn't I think of that?"

"God, why are you being so snarky?"

Mallory sighed and took another sip. "Sorry. Mother is driving me crazy. I shouldn't take it out on you."

"When's your house going to be finished?"

"Who knows? They've been saying in two weeks for the past two months."

"What made you decide to stay here?"

Mallory speared the green olive in her drink and then popped it in her mouth. "Mother insisted."

"I recall a time not too long ago when you would have told her to shove it."

"Yeah." With a wistful sigh, her sister's gaze went back to the window. "What's that guy's name, anyway?"

"I think it's Hector."

"Hmm." She thoughtfully sipped from her glass, her expression not one Tori liked. Mallory was in a reckless mood and clearly looking for trouble.

"Where's Mother?"

Mallory blinked and looked back at Tori. "At her monthly Garden Club luncheon meeting. Why do you think it's so peaceful around here?"

She smiled. "Yeah, I figured she was out."

"Yes, at the meeting, taking credit for all her award-winning roses that she didn't lift a finger to grow or nurture or do crap for." Mallory lifted her glass in salute before draining it and then frowning at Tori. "Doesn't it bother you that she does that? Look how many magazine spreads have featured *her* roses and the articles all make it sound like she slaves over those puppies."

"I honestly hadn't thought about it," she said, but the idea sank in and didn't sit well.

"Has Jake ever mentioned anything about it? I would think it would bother him and his father."

Tori's throat tightened. "What makes you think I talk to Jake?"

Mallory's lips curved in one of those annoying I-know-something-you-don't smiles she'd perfected when they were both teenagers. "What are you doing home, anyway?"

"I came to take you to lunch."

Her eyes widened. "Really?"

Tori nodded. "Really. Now, go brush your hair so I won't be ashamed to sit with you."

Mallory laughed, sounding like her old self. She put the glass in the sink. "Screw you."

"Screw you, too. Now hurry up before Mother gets home and we have to listen to a replay about how wonderful everyone thinks she is."

Mallory rolled her eyes. "You got it. Back in a flash."

"Oh, Mall." Tori was so relieved to see glimpses of the old Mallory that she had a great thought. "After lunch, I'd like you to go apartment shopping with me."

"Apartment shopping?" Her sister frowned. "For you?"

"Yep."

"No way."

"Way."

"You're moving out?"

"As soon as I can find a place."

A delighted look of deviltry gleamed from Mallory's eyes. "What did Mother say?"

"I haven't told her yet."

"Oh, boy, promise me you'll wait until I'm around to hear it when you do."

"Oh, honey, I'm sure that even if you're across town you'll still hear it."

Laughing, Mallory lingered in the doorway, just staring at Tori. "It's good to have you home."

"Right. So I can do all the work in the office."

The pleasure faded from Mallory's face. "I'd better go spruce up."

"Yeah. Go."

Tori waited until she heard Mallory head upstairs before she turned back to the window. Now would be an excellent time to talk to her sister about the drinking and the hopelessness Tori sensed. But she wouldn't do it. Not today.

Instead they would have a great lunch at La Griglia, then go buy new purses, Mallory's weakness, and then apartment shop. She'd call Karen, of course, and tell her she wouldn't be returning to the office. Nobody would miss her.

But right now Mallory needed her. And maybe she was being a coward by not bringing up the sensitive stuff, but just for now, it would be like old times.

# 8

JAKE SWUNG HIS BOOTED feet up on his desk and stared out of his office window. The room was small, big enough for a desk, two chairs and a couple of bookcases without leaving much butt room. Outside the door his secretary had a bigger office since she kept up all the filing and worked on the computer.

Although he hated the term secretary since she seemed more like an assistant, keeping him organized and on time, she was old school and insisted on the title. Said it looked better on her résumé. Like at sixty-four she needed it. Besides, he'd never let her quit. Hell, he'd promise to put her grandkids through college before he'd let her do that. He had the ideas but she was the guts of the operation, and fortunately for him, he was smart enough to know it.

He heard the phone ring in the outer office but ignored it knowing Selma would answer the call. If he thought for one moment it was Victoria, he would've grabbed it in a New York minute.

But she wouldn't call. Not her. Even if she knew how to find him she'd never call. Then again, maybe if she got horny enough...

Their whole relationship was about sex for her. Which didn't even constitute a relationship, he guessed. A couple of times he'd thought she'd softened toward him, but then the night would be over and she'd get dressed, all businesslike and leave with barely a goodbye.

What the hell, all he wanted was sex, too.

That's the only reason he was toying with the idea of calling her. To set something up for later. Or maybe he should give it a rest for a couple of nights. He hadn't been to the gym in a week. Work had gotten so crazy that his *Sports Illustrated* issues were piling up. He'd neglected stuff at the office, and Selma was going to chew him out royally.

As if he'd mentally summoned her, she poked her snow-white head inside his office. "Have you called Forever Green back yet?"

He sighed. "No."

"Then I assume you were just staring at the phone and thinking about doing it right now. Am I right?"

"Don't you have filing to do or something?"

She raised her brows. "Don't use that tone with me, young man. You don't get on the horn and treat this operation like a business I won't have any filing to do."

*Yeah, right.* He muttered under his breath and picked up the phone. But then couldn't find the pink message slip. "Selma!"

"Here." She brought it to him, and then folded her arms across her chest. "What's going on?"

"I'm calling just like you told me."

"You know damn well what I'm talking about. You've been grouchy and inattentive. Even Petey's been hiding the last two mornings when you came in."

"Good, that parakeet bugs me."

"Jake?"

"What?"

"Do you need to talk?"

"No."

She nodded. "Okay, if you change your mind, you know where I am."

He watched her go, still trim in crisp new blue jeans and a plaid cotton shirt, and wondered if he should introduce her to his father. Selma was full of life, playing golf on her days off, biking, volunteering at the library some evenings. She'd get the old man back into the mainstream, whether he liked it or not.

Jake smiled at the thought.

"I don't hear you talking," she hollered from her desk.

He grunted and picked up the phone. She was worse than his mother. The thought stopped him. He'd been six when she died. He barely remembered her.

Was that the reason for his special affection for Selma? Is that why he let her run roughshod over him when if anyone else dared to do that, he'd flatten them? Did she fill a need? Ridiculous. He was a grown man. Almost thirty-one. He didn't need a mother. Selma was a good secretary, that's all.

He picked up the receiver and punched in the numbers. When he got Roy Sutter's voice mail, Jake was almost relieved. He wasn't in the mood to talk about developing a new tool. After leaving a brief message, he redialed Victoria's office.

"VICTORIA WHITFORD."

"Hi, Tori, it's Kathryn. Sorry to call you at the office."

"No problem." She straightened, curious. "What's up?"

"I have a situation here. Not something I normally encourage but I have a client who wants to talk to you and no one else."

"Who?"

"Do you remember Beth with the long reddish hair down to her waist?"

"Of course. She arrived at the center last week with her two kids."

"Look, before I go any further I want you to know that I'm talking to you in the privacy of my office. If you don't want to talk to her, just say the word. I'll certainly understand and she'll never know I got a hold of you."

"Really, Kathryn, there's no problem."

"Okay, let me give you a brief rundown on what's happening. Her husband has given her an ultimatum that if she doesn't go home with the kids, he's going to file for divorce and custody in her absence. We both know how violent he is and what'll happen if she goes home."

"But she has the children with her. She has physical custody so he'd have to find them first. And then if he carried out that ridiculous threat, she wouldn't have to face him until they were in court, if it goes that far, right?"

"I tried to tell her that but she's so afraid of losing the children she isn't thinking straight. Apparently you made an impression that night you picked her up and brought her to the safe house and checked her in. Now she only wants to talk to you."

Tori glanced at her watch. Traffic would start getting really heavy in an hour. "I can be there in twenty-five minutes."

"No, you don't have to do that. I'll put her on the phone. She can talk in privacy."

"Don't you think it would be better to talk face-to-face?"

"To tell you the truth, she's wound so tight I'm not sure she'd wait the twenty-five minutes."

"Okay, put her on." Tori took several deep breaths as she waited, praying she'd say the right thing. Preaching didn't help, nor any hint of condemnation.

She remembered how fragile the woman had been the night Tori had picked her up from the hospital they used as a meeting point in order to safeguard the location of the center. Beth had already suffered a black eye and a cut on her arm that had required five stitches. Neither had been her first injury suffered at the hands of her abusive husband.

Tori had spent the rest of the night asking herself if she were cut out to do this kind of volunteering.

The experience had touched her deeply. She'd wanted to take Beth and her kids home with her, protect them from the stupid bastard who called himself husband and father. She'd wanted to rip his heart out with her bare hands.

But there were a lot more Beths out there, and Tori was slowly learning that the only way she could help was to listen and be a shoulder to cry on, and then help them maneuver the legal system if they wanted out. The problem was, few did. Out of fear of the unknown and a total lack of self-esteem, they kept going back to what was familiar.

She heard some rattling and then a deep breath over the phone line. "Tori?"

"Hey, Beth."

"Sorry, I know you're busy..." Her voice was soft and timid and utterly heartbreaking.

"Never too busy for you."

After a brief silence, she said, "I guess Kathryn told you what's going on."

"Some of it. Why don't you tell me yourself?"

She sighed heavily. "Clyde's gonna take my kids if I don't go home."

"How is he going to do that?" Tori asked calmly, remembering to keep her voice low and even, when she really wanted to go kick Clyde in the groin.

"What do you mean?"

"Does he know where you are? Have you told him where the center is?"

She gasped. "I'd never do that. I promised."

"So how would he get the children? They aren't in school yet. They're with you all the time."

"You don't know him, Tori. He's mean and ugly. He'll find a way." She sniffed. "Besides, he said he's sorry for cutting me. Says he won't do it again."

Tori really had to keep a tight reign on her emotions. She wanted to cry and scream at the same time. "But you've heard that before, Beth, haven't you?"

"Yes." Her voice was small yet defensive.

"Beth, do you want to go back to him?"

"No, but my kids—"

"Do you want them to see their daddy beating up on their mommy?"

She didn't answer, and Tori panicked. Had she gone too far? Had she lost Beth?

"No," Beth finally said. "But he knows people and he has money and I don't and if he files those legal papers there's nothing I can do."

"Well, I know people and I have money, and if he tries to lift a finger to take the children, I promise you he'll regret it for the rest of his sorry life." Tori closed her eyes and took a deep breath. Damn it. That was so not what she was supposed to say.

Beth giggled, and for a brief moment, Tori thought her stupidity was almost worth it.

"Hey, Beth?"

"I'm still here."

"You have to be strong. You have to want to change your situation or nothing will work. Do you understand?"

"I do wanna change things. It's just hard."

"I'd imagine getting beaten up all the time is harder."

"Yeah." Beth's voice caught on a sob.

"Would you do something for me?"

"What?"

"Do nothing. Just wait and see. You know he can't get to you and the children."

"But he could get one of them legal papers saying I kidnapped them. Judges don't like that."

"I bet Clyde told you that, right?"

Beth stayed silent.

"He's trying to bully you. Don't let him. Please, trust me. That's why you called, right? Because you trust me. I'm just asking you to trust me a little longer."

"Okay," Beth said, her voice a shade above a whisper. "Just don't let him take my kids."

Tori heard a clatter as Beth apparently laid down the phone. Since Beth hadn't hung up, Tori hoped that meant she was getting Kathryn back on the line. She waited and in a few seconds, Kathryn was back.

Tori explained the gist of the phone call, confessing to her stupidity, and then promised Kathryn that she would make good on her word to Beth. And that she would never get that personally involved again.

They hung up and Tori sank back in her chair, totally drained, feeling as if she'd just run a marathon. She stared at the ten-year forecast she'd been studying. It seemed incredibly insignificant.

Her line rang again. God, she hoped Beth hadn't

changed her mind. She lunged for the receiver, hoping to get it before Karen. "Yes?"

"Victoria?"

"Jake?"

"Am I catching you at a bad time?"

Her pulse still hadn't calmed down from the last call, and just hearing his voice sent it racing again. "No, I—I thought you were someone else."

"I hate calling you at the office but I figured that was better than calling you at home."

"No problem."

"I was wondering what you were doing tonight."

"Oh." Her gaze went to her desk calendar, her thoughts going haywire. Nothing was indicated but she kept a separate social calendar, and she knew she had something going on...a dinner she seemed to recall.

"Hey, if tonight's not good—"

"No, I was just thinking..." She remembered suddenly. The dinner her mother had planned with the Radcliffs. A late dinner, late enough that she could see Jake first. "Could we make it early?"

He didn't answer right away. Finally he said slowly, "Okay. Same place?"

"Sounds good." Her spirits lifted considerably. Time would be tight, meeting him and then getting to dinner on time, but she didn't care. After that last conversation, the thought of spending even ten minutes in his safe comforting arms made her giddy with relief.

"What time?"

"Six?" She glanced at her watch. "Even five-thirty if you can make it."

"That's in an hour. I doubt I'd be able to get across town by then. Let's make it six."

He hung up first, and she reluctantly set down the receiver. God, she couldn't wait to see him. After a boring morning of reading report after report, and then the emotional surge from talking with Beth, the sound of Jake's voice alone was like a warm breeze in January, a balm to her jittery nervous system.

She smiled as she sorted her papers. Already her mood had lifted. He'd help make everything all right.

Tori froze at the unexpected and totally inappropriate thought. Comforting her wasn't his job. Wasn't what she needed from him. It was about sex, she reminded herself. Only sex.

Her stomach started to knot and she had the sudden urge to grab her laptop and write the gang at Eve's Apple. Something felt wrong. Really wrong.

JAKE WASN'T SURPRISED she'd gotten to the hotel first. She'd seemed anxious. Idiotically the idea pleased him. That she'd wanted an early start was even more appealing. Maybe this time it wouldn't be so wham-bam-thank-you-ma'am.

He got off the elevator and went to the same room as last night. Observing the same courtesy she always extended, he knocked briefly before inserting the key card he'd picked up at the front desk, and then entered the room.

She was sitting on a chair, her legs curled under her, leafing through a magazine, dressed in a silky-looking red robe. Her clothes were laid over the other chair.

His heart thudded. The robe had to be hers. Was she planning on spending the night?

She looked up and smiled, wearing more makeup then usual. "Hi."

"You look terrific."

"Thank you." She uncurled her long gorgeous legs, exposing one shapely calf as she got to her feet. "Traffic was murder, wasn't it?"

"It's that time of day." He set the bottle of chardonnay he brought on the table. "Mind opening this while I undress?"

She seemed reluctant, but then nodded and picked up the corkscrew. Without saying a word or looking his way, she slowly uncorked the bottle.

"Something wrong?"

She jumped. "No. Nothing. I had a really bad day, that's all."

He pulled off his shirt and enjoyed the satisfaction of a long admiring look. "Anything you want to talk about?"

Her lips parted, but then she sealed them again and shook her head.

"Did I mention you look terrific?"

That got a smile out of her. "You don't have to flatter me. You know you're going to get lucky."

"Uh-huh." Instead of getting out of his jeans though, he went and got a glass out of the bathroom and poured some wine.

"What's wrong?"

He took a sip. It wasn't what she said so much as the blasé way in which she said it. "Nothing. Bad day, that's all."

At his mimicking, she stared at him, this stupid wounded look on her face. Like she wasn't the one who started the trouble. He sighed. "Okay, I'm sorry."

"Me, too." She looked down. "Maybe tonight wasn't a good idea. I really did have a shitty day and I—"

"Come here."

She looked up, her eyes startled.

"Come here," he repeated, and she took a step toward him.

"Let's start over."

Victoria let him take her hand. "Okay."

"I know a good way to do that."

She smiled. "I bet you do."

With his finger, he tilted her chin up. Her lips quivered slightly as he lowered his head. He kissed her lightly on one corner of her mouth and then the other. And then he drew back to look at her.

She flattened a palm against his chest, using the tip of her index finger to tease the skin around his nipple. He was insanely sensitive there, especially the left one, and she'd figured that out quickly.

He gritted his teeth, trying not to show any reaction, until he couldn't stand it another second and grabbed her wrist. She laughed, and he yanked the belt of her robe. The front fell open.

"Hey."

"Hey yourself." He cupped one of her bare breasts and greedily suckled it, until her gasp turned into a whimper.

In seconds she'd pulled off his jeans and boxers, and shrugged out of her robe. The red silk hit the floor and she tugged him toward the bed. It registered that she'd already turned down the covers, and her apparent eagerness inflated more than his ego.

He laid her down gently and then stretched out beside her, brushing back her hair so that he could kiss her neck. She wasted no time in reaching for him and wouldn't back down even when he tried to shift away.

"I want you inside of me," she whispered brokenly. "Now."

The fever in her voice and eyes inflamed him. He got a foil packet, then sheathed himself. She parted her legs and she was wet and sleek, and he easily slid inside.

She clenched her muscles around him and he threw back his head, willing himself to go slow. Impatient, she thrust her hips up causing an unbearable friction.

He lost control. Holding her hips, he plunged deeper inside, withdrew partially and plunged again, even deeper this time.

"Yes," she panted. "Yes."

He thought he'd explode. In ten seconds he did. She cried out again and he was a goner, climaxing like he never had in his life. He couldn't seem to stop coming. The more she clenched around him, the more control slipped away.

The experience stunned him. Weakened him so much that he finally rolled off to lie beside her, trying like hell to catch his breath. He listened to her labored breathing as they lay in silence, their thighs still touching, his arm draped over her waist.

Finally she stirred and rolled onto her side, facing him. She smiled. "Jake?"

"Yeah."

He stared at her, waiting for her to continue.

"Never mind."

"Come on."

She shook her head. "No, it's nothing. In fact, I forgot what I was going to say."

"Right."

She blushed, and snuggled against him so that he could no longer see her face.

He'd let her get away with it this time. "I have an idea."

"What's that?"

"How would you like to spend a week at a beach house in Galveston?"

She brought her head up. "With you?"

"Yeah."

"A whole week?"

"Thanks."

"No, I meant that I'd have to get out of work and I have this other thing I do some evenings. A week's a long time."

"Never mind." He mentally kicked himself for

bringing it up. Talk about caught up in the moment. The thought of waking up together each morning and then having the time to get to know each other better had seemed so damn appealing. "It was just an idea."

"No, wait." Excitement lit her eyes and she pushed herself up on her elbow. "I haven't really started anything meaty at work. It's just a bunch of reading so far." Her brows drew together in a slight frown and she chewed at her lower lip. "Can I think about it? Let you know tomorrow."

He shrugged. "Sure."

"Great." She turned over and then rolled off the bed. "Will you call me, or shall I call you?"

"Either way." He watched her walk toward the bathroom. "I'll give you my cell number."

She stopped and picked up her clothes. "I'll leave you my cell number, too."

"What are you doing?"

She looked at him in surprise. "Oh, I have a dinner to go to in an hour. Sort of a blind date my mother set up." She rolled her eyes before disappearing into the bathroom.

He stared at the closed door, feeling like he'd just been sucker punched.

# 9

"SCREW HER." Jake slammed his desk drawer. He still couldn't get over Victoria coming out and telling him she had a date, as if Jake were that inconsequential. "I don't need that shit."

"What shit?"

He looked up to find Hector standing at his office door. "What are you doing here?"

"I came to get my check, *amigo*. Where's Selma?"

"At lunch."

"The rest of the boys are in the truck. They want to get to the bank before the crowd. She always has them ready by now."

Jake muttered a curse as his gaze drew to the stack of checks Selma had left for him to sign. He'd totally forgotten about them. "I've got them over here. Give me a couple of minutes to sign them."

"Okay." Hector walked in and made himself comfortable on one of the chairs opposite Jake. "Who were you talking to when I came in?"

"Myself." Jake got out his pen and started signing each check while ignoring Hector.

"Did you answer?"

"Shut up."

The other man laughed. "Must be a woman."

Jake frowned at him. "What are you talking about?"

"You going loco again, *amigo*. Talking to yourself. No sense of humor. Your chin touching your chest."

He went back to signing checks, each signature an angry scrawl. "It has nothing to do with a woman, okay?"

"Okay," Hector said, sounding unconvinced. "If you say so."

"Here." He handed him the checks. "What about the Whitford place? Anything I should know about?"

"Nah, the old lady was inspecting the yellow roses by the pond when I got there this morning, but she didn't say nothing. She disappeared as soon as I parked the truck." He got to his feet. "Man, that woman needs to get laid. She always looks like she's sucking a lemon."

Jake sighed. His father would have a stroke if he heard Hector talking like that about Mrs. Whitford. "All right, get out of here."

"Yes, sir, boss." Hector stopped at the door and grinned. "Hope your woman troubles turn out okay."

Jake had the juvenile urge to flip him off. Instead he buried his face in the quarterly statement he needed Selma to send to the accountant by the end of next week. None of the figures made sense. He was still too busy steaming over Victoria.

As soon as he heard the front door close, he brought his head up and threw down the pen. He should have asked Hector about the Warren job. Contractually they were bound to finish the landscaping by mid-October. It was a huge project that, if completed satisfactorily, promised many more lucrative contracts with other malls.

Jake wasn't as interested in expanding the business as he probably should be. But the four-man crew who worked under Hector consisted of his brother, two cousins and a friend, and they all needed the work.

Damn that Victoria.

He couldn't get her out of his head. Even in the middle of something—a phone conversation, or reconciling an invoice, she'd just pop up. What made him really angry was that he couldn't remember letting anyone get to him this way.

So why her? Yeah, the sex was phenomenal. But the aggravation wasn't worth it. That's what bothered him the most. His own stupidity. He knew he wasn't in her league, and she'd made no effort to sugarcoat what she wanted from him. Maybe it was that whole thing about her being a Whitford, someone unattainable, that had him continuing to sniff around.

His gaze went to the phone. A week of great sex was nothing to turn your nose up at. It had nothing to do with pride. They were using each other for the sex.

*Shit!*
Screw her. No way would he call.


To: The Gang at Eve's Apple
From: Angel@EvesApple.com
Subject: SOS
I think I'm in trouble, guys. He wants me to spend a week with him at a beach house. So far, we haven't spent more than three hours with each other. And that was only once. A week of great sex wouldn't be a problem. Except that he's really nice. No, skip nice. Exciting, funny, the best lover in the world, and he seems to genuinely want to know about me, even like how my day was.

Last night I almost told him about a problem I was having at this place where I volunteer. He doesn't even know I go there after work. Doesn't need to know. Too much information. Right? It's not as if we have a relationship. We have sex and then get up and get dressed and go. Sort of.

Damn, I think I'm in over my head. I might like him too much. I don't think I should go to the beach house. Too personal. Of course I don't think it's HIS beach house, but a whole week? I dunno...
Help!
Angel


To: Angel at Eve's Apple
From: Kelly@EvesApple.com
Subject: SOS
Relax, kiddo. I think you're getting too hyper for

nothing. Sorry I haven't written for a week but I've been out of town, but I caught up on all your e-mails last night. What's one lousy week? You said the sex was great. Go for it. If you think things will get too complicated, maybe you could suggest going for only three days.

Love,

Kelly

p.s. What's up with going to a hotel? I didn't catch your answer.

Why was everyone so damn concerned about them meeting at a hotel? Sheesh. She reread the e-mail and then stared blankly at it, thinking about what Kelly had said. She had a point. Maybe three days was doable. Tori could take paperwork with her. Get the reports read during the day. They didn't have to spend twenty-fours a day in each other's faces.

She sighed. But he had such a nice face. Enigmatic dark eyes, full sensual lower lip, a strong jaw. Great smile.

Oh, God, this was not a good idea. Three hours had been enough to distract her. Three days spelled addiction.

She scrolled down, desperate for more advice, and hoping one of the others had written, as well. Tori smiled. Good old Taylor had come through.

To: Angel at Eve's Apple
From: Taylor@EvesApple.com

Subject: Stop and smell the roses
Okay, I don't get it. If you like this guy, what's the problem? Why not take a week to see what happens? Who knows? Maybe you'll find you have a lot in common. Maybe you'll end up like Ben and me. :)

Go, Angel, or you'll always wonder. Always. You know I'm right. Besides, how much work do you think you'll get done knowing you could have been lounging on some beach, having the best sex of your life?

Good luck, kid.
Love,
Taylor


Sighing, Tori checked to see if either of the Barbaras had written. Neither one had, so she decided to send another message. How much to say was the tricky part. The gang didn't understand her dilemma because they didn't know the whole story. She hadn't wanted to reveal too much and blow her anonymity. But the more she got to know the gang, the more comfortable she became, and consequently she recognized the ludicrousness of her paranoia.

She thought about it for a moment, how all her life her mother had drilled into her and Mallory how they were different from other people. That it was imperative that they kept their lives private. Their father had a high profile in the business world, and Mother had an equally prominent name in the society columns.

Tori understood from an early age that she had a

responsibility to protect the Whitford name, to contribute to the success of the multigenerational company developed by Tori's great-great-grandfather.

Jake could never be a part of that life. He'd hate every moment of the pomp and circumstance that surrounded her world. Sure, she'd been mildly defiant, by using a nickname and working at the center, but mostly she avoided confrontation. Her mother could be unbearably intolerant and outspoken, and if Tori were to introduce Jake into the...

She shuddered at the thought.

That could never happen. It would be awful. Any connection they had would be destroyed.

She started another e-mail, trying to capture her dilemma in words. After typing three sentences, she stared at the screen in horror. Her mother sounded like a tyrant, and Tori sounded like a whipped puppy. The gang would never understand her family dynamic.

Tori took in a deep breath, her head beginning to swim. She wasn't sure she understood, either. The whole thing was so damn complicated.

She closed her eyes, the week away starting to sound better and better. Or even as Kelly had suggested, three or four days were better than nothing. If everything went all right, they could stay longer.

The answer suddenly seemed crystal clear. She signed off and closed her laptop. Next, she called Kathryn to check up on Beth, who'd thankfully remained at the center. Tori explained to Kathryn she'd be out of town for a few days and left her cell phone number.

After disconnecting the call, she swallowed around the lump that had been building in her throat, took a deep breath and then punched in Jake's number.

"OH, MY, GOD, this is awesome." Tori leaned over the deck railing of the sprawling beach house and gazed out at the sailboats on the Gulf, the only sign of civilization for miles. "This couldn't be a more perfect day."

Jake shaded his eyes and stared up at the cloudless blue sky and privately agreed. Already his mood had improved. When she'd called the day before, he'd almost told Victoria to go to hell. Let her mother find her a rich boyfriend to take her for a getaway weekend.

But something stopped him. He just couldn't do it. After all, what red-blooded male would turn down great sex? That's the only thing that had stopped him from blowing her off.

"Can we go sailing?" she asked, turning to him, her eyes shining with a childlike excitement that disarmed him. "I've never been."

"No kidding?"

She shrugged. "I never had the opportunity. My parents aren't exactly water sports kind of people."

"Where did you go on vacations?"

She frowned. "You mean, with them?"

He nodded, some of the resentment he'd held on to on the drive down beginning to slip away.

She looked away, focusing on the water gently lapping the sandy beach. "We never really had family vacations. My dad has always worked a lot and, well, Mother traveled but not to places for children. Mostly spas or garden shows, that sort of thing. We had a nanny that used to take Mallory and I to the symphony in Dallas on occasion."

The symphony? Yeah, right, that was on his wish list as a child. By the time he'd been twelve, he and his sister had both been to Disneyland twice with their dad. They'd also visited Six Flags Magic Mountain a couple of times. They'd only be away for four days tops, and it wasn't until much later that he realized it must have been hard financially on his father, but he never once let it show. Family vacations had been important to him. Important enough that he'd even leave the precious Whitford grounds for a few days.

He looked back at Victoria. "Have you ever been to Disneyland?"

She blinked at him. "No."

"Any kind of amusement park?"

She shook her head.

"We're going to Disneyland," he said, the impulse obviously surprising her as much as himself.

"Now?"

He chuckled. "Next time."

She started to smile, and then panic flickered in her eyes and she suddenly got real interested in studying the outside architecture. "You haven't shown me the house yet."

He got the message. Loud and clear. There wasn't going to be any next time. "Let's go."

At the gruffness in his voice, she slid him a wary look and then preceded him into the house. He left the sliding glass door open to let in the breeze. The house had been closed up for some time. In fact, it had sat vacant while it had been on the market for the past year.

"I like the way the architect did this," she said, twirling around to look at it from every angle. "One big room for the kitchen and dining room and family room. Perfect for a party. Or even just cooking and watching TV. Plus you can see the Bay from three sides."

"Yeah, you can also see the water from two of the three bedrooms. Even the third one lets you get a small glimpse. Come on, I'll show you."

She followed him down the short hall. "You haven't told me who owns this place."

"The bank, probably."

She laughed. "Come on, really."

He opened a door. "This is the master bedroom."

Her lips parted as she entered the semicircular room. Glass and a wooden deck separated them from the beach. There were more windows than walls.

He had to admit, the view was spectacular. Even at night when all the stars were out, the moon golden, you could sometimes see ships traveling in the distance, lights strung from brow to stern.

"This is incredible." She stood at the glass doors,

shaking her head. "I don't understand why someone isn't living here."

"Too far a commute if you work in Houston. Besides, would you ever want to go to work at all?"

She grinned. "And your point would be?"

"Yeah, right, like you don't live for work."

Her eyebrows came down. "That is one thing no one can accuse me of."

"Right."

She gave him a peeved look. "I'm not talking about work for the next fours days. I'm not even thinking about it. Got it?"

"Then why bring the briefcase?"

Color rose in her cheeks. "Appearances," she said tightly, and when he frowned she added, "Look, I just started the job and I have a ton of reports to read in order to familiarize myself with the company. I kind of told my father I was getting away in order to catch up without distraction."

He smiled. "Is that right?"

"You don't understand." She tuned back to stare out the window. "I do have a responsibility to contribute to the business."

"Actually I was thinking about the distraction part." He moved closer and slipped his arms around her waist, drawing her back against his chest. "You don't think you'll have any distraction here?" he asked, and slid his hands up to cup her breasts.

She stiffened. "Can people see inside?"

"No."

"Sure?"

"Positive."

With a sigh, she relaxed against him. "How do you know? Bring many women here?"

"You're the first." He turned her around and kissed her, first on the tip of her nose and then on the lips. Gently, teasingly. "Come here."

When she realized he was leading her to the bed, she put on the brakes. "We can't use this room."

"Why not?"

"This has to be the owner's room."

"He won't care."

"But Jake—

Ignoring her protests, he pulled up the hem of her knit shirt and got it over her head. The peach-colored bra she wore had a front clasp and was easily freed and discarded. He stopped and stared at the beauty of her firm, round breasts, the rosy tips of her nipples.

Nibbling at her lower lip, she glanced out the window. "How far away are the neighbors?"

"Too far to hear you scream."

She sharply brought her gaze back to him, excitement already sparkling in her eyes. "Are you going to make me scream?"

He smiled, and unzipped her shorts.

# 10

TORI LAY ON HER SIDE, adjusted the sheet to cover her breasts, and watched him sleep. She wasn't sure he actually was asleep but with his deep, even breathing and the rise and fall of his chest, she thought it was a safe guess. Safe enough that she considered furtively working the sheets down below his waist so she could get her fill of him.

Out of the corner of her eye, a bright red and yellow sail close to shore caught her attention. Being surrounded by so much glass was an incredible experience, as if she were on the beach herself.

When she looked back at him, he was watching her.

She snuggled into the pillow. "You're awake."

He gave her one of those slow lazy smiles that caused way too much reaction. "I wasn't asleep."

"Yeah, right."

"*You* were."

She made a face. "I was not."

"For about ten minutes. Not exactly snoring but—"

"I do not snore."

"Let me finish. It was more like a soft purr."

"You're dreaming."

Chuckling, he reached for her. "This better not be a dream," he said and pulled her against him.

Amazingly he was already getting hard, and she automatically moved her hips.

"So you haven't had enough," he murmured.

"If it's too soon for you, no problem," she said all innocent and taunting.

He let out a low growl, and grabbing her wrists, pinned her to the mattress.

She giggled at the slight roughness of his chin as he nuzzled her neck. "Ooh, I like it when you get all Neanderthal on me."

He looked up to give her a wicked lift of his brow. "Then you're gonna love this." He jerked off the sheet, ignoring her yelp of surprise, and pulled her thighs apart.

"There's a boat right out front." She tried to squirm away as he maneuvered himself between her legs. "I'm sure they can see inside."

"They can't." He put his mouth on her, using only the tip of his tongue and light torturous strokes to drive her mad.

She sank back into the pillows and closed her eyes. When he spread her nether lips, she briefly tensed. But his tongue worked its magic and the tingling started building astonishingly fast.

"Jake, please."

He wouldn't stop. Not that she was certain she wanted him to. But if he didn't, it would all be over so...

# Get FREE BOOKS and a FREE GIFT when you play the...

## LAS VEGAS

### GAME

*Just scratch off the gold box with a coin. Then check below to see the gifts you get!*

**YES!** I have scratched off the gold Box. Please send me my **2 FREE BOOKS** and **gift for which I qualify.** I understand that I am under no obligation to purchase any books as explained on the back of this card.

**350 HDL DZ94**　　　　　　　**150 HDL D2AK**

FIRST NAME　　　　　　　LAST NAME

ADDRESS

APT.#　　　　　CITY

STATE/PROV.　　　　ZIP/POSTAL CODE　　　　(H-B-07/04)

| 7 | 7 | 7 | Worth TWO FREE BOOKS plus a BONUS Mystery Gift! |

Worth TWO FREE BOOKS!

TRY AGAIN!

**www.eHarlequin.com**

Too late.

Wave after wave of spasms overcame her. Heat spread through her belly and chest. She couldn't catch her breath. It was too much, so intense it was frightening. She pushed at his head to get him to stop. He wouldn't back off, and she lay back, drowning, the sensation so incredibly complete that she nearly wept.

JAKE STOOD at the open refrigerator door, squinting at the contents before grabbing a package of cheese, mayonnaise and some roast beef wrapped in deli paper. He was pretty sure he'd forgotten something, but damn if he could think of it now. "I didn't know what kind of stuff you liked so I got a little variety."

"I didn't even think about food." Tori walked into the kitchen in a white robe, her hair still wet. "Sorry. I should have picked something up, too."

"Don't worry about it. We have enough for at least three days and if we need anything else there's a store less than two miles away. What do you think about sandwiches for dinner?"

"I'm starved. Crackers and water even sounds good."

"Me, too." They'd both worked up an appetite, all right. Hell, he hoped he could make it through the four days without shriveling up. "We have roast beef, ham and turkey. What's your pleasure?"

"I like all three. Whatever you're having, I'll have. Did you get tomatoes and lettuce?" She came to stand beside him and check out the fridge. She smelled so damn good.

"Yep, I remembered both."

"Good boy, now, please tell me you brought dessert."

He reared his head back and gave her a mock look of surprise. "But darlin', you already had dessert."

"Hey, I'm serious." She bent to look more closely into the refrigerator.

His gaze drifted to the lapels of her robe where a gap gave him a glimpse of one plump breast. His body reacted immediately.

Food first. They really needed to eat. Especially if he expected to go another couple of rounds tonight.

"We have nothing sweet, do we?" she asked, her pouty lips distracting him again.

"Oh, honey, you are—"

"Never mind." She put up a silencing hand, and sighed. "Don't say it. Let's eat."

"Yes, ma'am." He got out the lettuce and tomato, and set them next to the cheese and meat on the counter.

"Mustard, too, please," she said as she got down plates.

"On roast beef?"

"Yes, mixed with mayonnaise."

He made a sound of disgust.

"Have you ever tried it?" She kept opening drawers until she found a knife and spoon.

"No."

"Then you how can you have an opinion?"

"Ever try S&M?" He brought out the mustard.

She rolled her eyes.

He smiled. "Come here."

"What?"

"Come here, and I'll show you."

Her narrowed gaze went to his bare chest, and then lowered to where his jeans rode just below his navel. She moistened her lips. "I thought we were making sandwiches."

"We are."

"So why do you need me over there?"

He leaned a hip against the counter. "I like to watch you walk."

She laughed. "Very funny."

"Believe me, funny is the last thing I'm trying to be."

She tilted her head slightly to the side as if trying to figure him out. "What is it about my walk that blows up your skirt?"

He chuckled. "Okay, you caught me. It's not the walk. It's the robe."

"The robe?" She looked down and discovered that the belt had loosened and that a couple steps would probably have caused it to fall open. Laughing and cinching the belt, she looked back up at him. "Get the bread."

"Yes, ma'am."

She made up her mustard/mayo while he washed and sliced the tomatoes. They continued to work together, until two fat sandwiches were made, his without lettuce and mayo only. He brought a bag of chips to the table, half expecting her to refuse them, but she eagerly grabbed a handful and put them on her plate.

He smiled, and dug into his sandwich.

"Hey, don't forget to at least try this." She shoved the mustard concoction toward him.

It looked pretty bad. "I wouldn't make you eat that."

"I won't *make* you, but..." Her lips curved in a mischievous smile. "If you try it, I'll be your slave for five minutes."

The yellow mixture looked better already. "Ten."

"Six."

"Nine."

She glared at him. "Seven is my final offer. I mean it."

"Eight."

"Fine." She spooned up a heap.

"But I don't have to put it in my sandwich, right?"

Her sigh was pure disgust. "Dip a chip in it or use your finger if you want. But it's much better in the— What are you doing?"

He came around the table and using his little finger, smeared the mixture across her lower lip. And then he lowered his head and licked it off. "Mmm, you're right. Pretty tasty."

She gave her head a small shake of disbelief. "Go back to your chair."

"Yes, ma'am."

"Seriously, isn't it good?" She put a chip in her mouth and then licked the salt off her lips.

"Better than I thought, I'll give you that."

Her lips lifted in a triumphant smile. "Would I steer you wrong?"

He grinned back. "Listen, you aren't going to be steering me anywhere. For the next eight minutes, you'll do exactly as I tell you."

"WE CAN'T SPEND the whole four days in bed," Tori said, as she lay partially atop him, her cheek pressed to his chest, listening to the steady rhythm of his heart. Idly she swirled her fingers through the hair starting on his chest, tapering to his navel, and watched the sun set over the water from the bedroom window.

"Why not?"

She smiled. Not a bad question. "Because."

"Could you be a little more specific?"

She yanked a chest hair.

"Ouch." He reached around and lightly pinched her bare bottom.

Giggling, she squirmed to a semiupright position, using her elbow to brace herself. "Okay, truce."

"Truce. Don't go." He pulled her back against him, and she gladly reclaimed her spot against his chest.

Just lying beside him, skin touching skin, his heartbeat strong and steady against her, filled her with such utter contentment that she knew she should be worried. She should be packing her things and headed back to Houston. But that was the thing about contentment, it paralyzed her. Made her push back the crazy, nagging thoughts that once down this road, she'd never find her way home again.

"Don't worry," he said, squeezing her a little tighter. "We can't stay in bed the whole time. We'll have to go shopping."

"For what?"

"Food."

"We have a refrigerator full of stuff."

"I'm guessing only enough for the next two days. I didn't know you ate so much."

She brought her head up sharply and bumped his chin.

"Ouch!" He half groaned, half laughed.

"You pain in the ass." She tried to get away but he kept his arms banded round her. "I thought we called a truce."

"That wasn't a jab. I like a woman who doesn't poke her food around her plate."

"Let go of me."

"Nope."

"I mean it."

"You sure?" He withdrew long enough to force her onto her back, and then he nuzzled her neck.

"I'm going to count to three..."

He drew back and looked at her in surprise. "You don't seriously think I was taking a shot at you."

"I don't know." She shrugged feeling sheepish suddenly. "No. I'm just sensitive about my weight."

"Why?" His expression of total disbelief soothed her.

"Not in general. It's just that I put on five or six

pounds the last two weeks of school." Damn it. Why had she brought it up? Why hadn't she just let the remark go? What did she care what he thought?

"Where?"

"Excuse me?"

"Where? Here?" He ran his hand over her belly, up between her rib cage. "No, that can't be the place." He cupped one breast and then the other. "Can't be here. These are perfect."

She giggled and swatted his hand. "What are you doing?"

"Hmm." He frowned, pursed his lips. "Maybe here," he said and ran his palm over her hip and then slid his hand behind to cup her bottom. "Can't find anything, though I can't say I'm not enjoying the search."

She tried to keep a straight face. "You're a piece of work, you know that?"

"Darlin', do you think that's the first time I've heard that?"

"Not for a second."

He smiled. "Where was I? Ah..." He molded his palm down her outer thigh, and she winced, knowing exactly what he'd discovered. "Nice."

"How diplomatic."

"Are you disagreeing with me?" He looked at her with such comical disbelief that she had to smile. "Who do you think is the bigger connoisseur of the female thigh?"

She shook her head, and rolled her eyes.

"Come on. You're a knockout and you know it."

Her heart jumped. "You've been out in the sun too long."

"You're right. The heat's made me a little mad." Growling, he playfully bit the side of her neck.

It tickled like crazy but no matter how much she squirmed he wouldn't let up. His hands started another trek up her body and the anticipation of what he'd do next had her holding her breath. His exploration not only excited her but his reaction touched a special place in her heart.

Silly physical attributes meant nothing, she knew, but his acceptance did. While growing up, any type of praise had been a precious commodity. Nothing was said when she'd won a piano recital or got straight A's. Attention was garnered only when she hadn't lived up to her parents' standards.

Jake accepted her, warts and all. Of course it behooved him to stay in her good graces if just for the sex. That idea bothered her. It shouldn't, but it did.

"Hey," she said, before she started thinking too much. "What about this grocery shopping you mentioned?"

He cocked an eyebrow at her. "You want to talk about our grocery list?"

"Yeah."

"Now?"

"We definitely need more cheese. And tomatoes."

He snorted and fell back to stare at the ceiling. "I think I should be offended."

"Poor baby. I didn't mean to bruise your ego." She stroked his chest.

"Lower." He turned to her and grinned. "If you're looking for my ego."

She laughed and promptly withdrew her hand. "I'm getting dressed."

"Now I'm really hurt."

She paused at the edge of the bed. "Don't be. You wore me out. I need to refuel. So do you." She got up. "A tuna sandwich okay for dinner?" she asked, glancing over her shoulder.

His appreciative gaze was centered on her backside. A moment's discomfort quickly passed. There was no censure in his eyes. He was very obviously enjoying the view.

She picked up her robe, slid it on and left without waiting for an answer, unwilling to dispel the warm fuzzy feeling of being appreciated. She loved the sexy beautiful way he made her feel. The way he allowed her to overlook the flaws and enjoy the good things.

God help her. It had to stop.

"THAT IS SOME PRETTY FUNKY-looking cheese." Jake frowned at the sizable chunk Victoria had thrown in the cart next to the fresh loaf of French bread.

"It's plain old blue cheese." She barely looked up, too busy studying the label on a package of reduced-fat white cheddar.

"I've had blue cheese dressing many times and it never looked like that."

She gave him a puzzled look. "Are you trying to be funny?"

"No."

"Well, wait until you try it, especially mixed with cream cheese as a dip. You'll love it."

He doubted that. Sometimes rich people had peculiar tastes. What the hell was wrong with garden-variety onion dip? They had tons of those little cartons for sale so obviously a lot of people liked it. Not that he cared what she bought. He just liked messing with her. He liked the way her brows puckered and drew together ever so slightly whenever she didn't know whether to take him seriously or not.

She'd always hesitate, and study his face before replying. She wasn't quick to shoot off her mouth. He liked that, too. Her keen sense of humor was another trait that pleased him. She enjoyed a good joke and had no problem laughing at herself.

"For the record, I don't like reduced fat cheeses, either," he said leaning on the cart, watching her study the label.

"Oh..." She lifted a brow. "Which ones have you had?"

"If I don't like something, why would I eat it?

She smiled sweetly, and tossed the package into the cart. "You'll love this one."

An older woman with short white hair passed them, a grin tugging at her bright pink lips. To her they probably sounded like an old married couple. That would really be something. Him married to Victoria. Sunday dinners at the Whitfords' mansion. Having a brandy in the study with *the* Harrison Whitford.

*Yeah, right.*

"We'd better get some fruit, and maybe cereal. What kind do you like?" She stopped at the next aisle, one hand resting on the cart as she studied the signage.

She looked oddly domestic, a grocery list in one hand, a pen to cross off items in the other. Except she didn't look like the other moms and wives in the store. Dressed in jeans and a polo shirt, with the sleeves of a sweater tied casually around her shoulders she looked stylish, chic. Her posture was perfectly straight as were her teeth. Even with the god-awful humidity her hair looked perfect.

Other men eyed her, which was natural, but even women often gave her a second look. To her credit, she didn't seem to want the attention. In fact, she didn't seem to notice it. But there was definitely something about her that shouted she was different.

It was probably nothing more than the casual grace of the rich. The old-money rich. The generation so accustomed to the finer things in life they didn't feel the need to broadcast their social stature. They accepted good fortune as their due, and blithely wore their wealth and power like an old comfortable sweater.

That described Victoria exactly.

"Jake?"

He snapped out of his reverie and looked at her. She smiled. "Daydreaming?"

"Yeah."

"Then I guess you didn't hear my question about the cereal."

"Wheaties," he said. "We'll need our strength."

Laughing, she glanced around, and then gave him a fierce glare. "Stop it."

"Yes, ma'am." He gave her a smart salute that had her rolling her eyes before she started down the aisle.

He didn't blame her one bit. Not the way she dressed or carried herself. She had been born into money. This was who she was.

Unfortunately it reminded him of who he wasn't, of why she'd left his bed to go on more suitable dates. Maybe that's why he liked it best when they lay naked, stripped of unpleasant reminders. Just the two of them, a man and a woman, pleasing each other without pretense.

And when the whim had passed? What then? They'd go their separate ways. Anger erupted from the pit of his stomach, and gripped him with a restlessness he didn't understand.

"Victoria?"

She turned to him with a sweet smile.

"We have to go."

Her face clouded. "What's wrong?"

"Nothing." He took the box of cereal from her hands and put it in the cart. She looked so confused that he forced a smile and whispered, "We have important business at home."

"Business?"

He nodded slowly.

Her eyes widened slightly as his meaning registered, and then she smiled and led him to the checkout line.

# 11

"LET'S EAT OUT HERE on the deck tonight." Tori let her head roll to the side to look at Jake sprawled out on the lounge chair beside her.

He gave her a lazy smile that set her tummy fluttering. "A sunset dinner? Sounds good."

She sighed with contentment and closed her eyes. How could two days have already passed? If the next two flew by as quickly, she wouldn't be ready to return to Houston. Not by a long shot. Though neither of them had said anything about staying the full week, she was ready to say the hell with it and stay a month if he wanted.

"I have a question."

She looked over at him, surprised to find him watching her. "What's that?"

"Where do you see yourself in ten years?"

The question took her aback. Laughing, she shook her head. "I have trouble planning next month's schedule."

"I'm not talking about planning or short-term goals. We all have visions of our futures. Where we want to be at say, thirty and then forty, fifty and so on..."

She turned to watch the gulls soaring over the water, dipping occasionally, in search of fish. She'd sound obtuse if she told him the truth, that she honestly hadn't projected that far into the future. It wasn't as if she had many choices.

"If that was too personal, I apologize for overstepping my bounds."

She frowned at the hint of sarcasm in his voice. "It's not that I find it too personal. I honestly don't know what to say. I've always known I'd work for my father. He probably hopes I learn enough that some day he can turn over the reigns just like his father did." She shrugged helplessly and darted him a sheepish look. "To tell you the truth, I'm embarrassed that I don't have a better or wittier answer."

He regarded her with such intense curiosity and disbelief she was ready to get up and go inside when he finally spoke. "You've been brainwashed."

That startled a laugh out of her. "Brainwashed? What's in that iced tea you're drinking?"

He blinked, stared at her for another second, and then his lips curved into a smile. Ironically it made him look rather sad. "What about marriage, kids, going to school reunions every ten years, that whole thing?"

She exhaled slowly. "I like kids. I think. I haven't been around too many." She thought about the children who went to stay at the shelter with their mothers, most of them shy and quiet, almost as if they wanted to be invisible. "They're an awfully big responsibility."

"Yes, they are. Do your parents expect you to give them grandchildren?"

"I suppose." She laughed at the idea of her mother in the role of grandmother.

Jake smiled. "What?"

"I was just picturing my mother stooping down to kiss dirty little faces. Not."

He shared her laughter. "Yeah, pretty hard to imagine, all right."

She started to relax again, enjoying the warmth of the sun on her face. "I wonder if Mallory is thinking about having a baby. She and Richard have been married for almost three years."

"I take it you two don't talk much."

"Not since I've been back." Without a second thought, she added, "Coming home again has been really weird." She stopped and glanced over at him. This was getting personal.

"You want to explain?"

"Not really."

"Okay." He turned his face toward the sun and closed his eyes.

She had the most idiotic feeling that she'd offended him or let him down in some way. "I mean it's no big deal. I don't think anyone else would understand."

"Try me."

Tori sighed. "It mainly has to do with my mother. Either she's changed, or I'm not as tolerant."

"Probably a little of both. You've experienced independence. Your relationship had to change."

"True." She let it go at that. As annoyed as she was with her mother, she didn't want to discuss what a domineering snob she'd become. "What about your sister? Does she have kids?"

His face lit up. "A boy. His name is Tommy. What a little spitfire. He keeps Sally on her toes. She says she's waiting until he's four before she has another one."

"Uncle Jake, huh?"

"Yeah." The way he beamed tugged at her heart, showed her a whole new side to him.

"What about you? Want any rug rats of your own?"

"Definitely.

"Really?"

"Why the surprise?"

"Oh, I don't know." She grinned. "I guess none of my fantasies of you included children."

"I'm hurt."

"Hey, I was a kid myself when I was daydreaming about you."

"And now?"

"No more fantasies. I have the real thing."

One side of his mouth lifted. "You should be in politics."

She laughed breezily, knowing full well his remark spoke to her sidestepping of the question. "I guess your father is happy he at least has Tommy."

"Yeah, but he doesn't get to see him enough. Sally and her family lives in Oregon. Dad sees them maybe twice a year."

"What a shame."

Jake shrugged. "That's partly his fault. He should have retired already. Then he could see them as much as he wanted."

"Retire? He's too young."

"Not for the kind of work he does."

"Maybe." Tori shook her head. "He loves poking around the garden. What would he do?"

"Hell, I'll fix him up with my secretary. She'll keep him plenty busy."

"Your secretary?"

"Yeah, she's a widow," he said matter-of-factly and shaded his eyes to look out over the bay. "Look at that boat coming in from the east. What a honey."

Tori stared at him. "Why do you have a secretary?"

"The same reason most people do. She keeps me organized." He followed the course of the boat. "Looks like she's docking at the place next door. I'd like to get a closer look. Want to go for a walk?"

"There isn't a next door. That house has to be a half mile away."

"Wuss."

She made a face at him. "I'm not afraid of a little exercise but it's—" She stopped to listen, thinking she heard a familiar ring from inside. "That's my cell phone," she said, quickly getting to her feet.

"They'll leave a message."

"No. I have to get this." God, she hoped she'd done the right thing by encouraging Beth to call if she needed her. It didn't matter. What mattered now was that Tori be available. She fumbled with the sliding glass door but got inside and answered in the nick of time.

"Tori?"

She recognized the timid voice. "Beth?"

"I'm sorry to bother you—"

"No bother at all." Tori turned to check if she'd closed the door behind her. Not that Jake was listening. He'd gotten off the lounger and was leaning over the deck railing. "How are you?"

Beth sniffled. "Not good."

"What's wrong?"

"He sent me papers."

"Your husband?"

"Yes," Beth whispered. "They look real important and legal-like. It says I'm supposed to give him the children by Monday or I go to jail."

Tori kept her gaze on Jake. He started looking impatient, shooting glances over his shoulder toward the door. "Did he send them himself, or are they from a lawyer?"

"Well, it's in his handwriting."

Tori sighed with relief. "Is it on legal stationery?"

Silence.

"Beth, have you shown the papers to Kathryn?"

"No, she's been in court with Mary Therese all day."

The door opened. Tori jumped.

Jake frowned at her.

"Hold on a moment," she said to Beth. "Stay on the line, okay?" She got Beth's promise and then held the phone away from her mouth. "You go on ahead," she said to Jake. "I'll catch up or meet you back here."

"I'll wait."

"No. Go." She didn't mean to sound so sharp but she didn't want Beth hanging up.

He sent her a curious look before closing the glass door.

She had to let it go. She'd promised Beth she wouldn't abandon her. If it meant she had to return to Houston early, Jake would just have to understand.

DINNER OUT ON THE DECK was pretty quiet. Jake knew it was his fault. He'd acted like a two-year-old earlier. He knew her job was important to her. So what if she got one stinking call? She hadn't been interested in that cabin cruiser, anyway. That was his deal.

The solitary walk over to the neighbors had done him good. Helped put the long weekend into perspective. Yeah, he was getting to know her better, but that didn't mean anything. All this getaway was about was making the sex easier. No dashing across town to get to a hotel, and then skipping out in two hours.

He should be grateful. She made the affair easy. So why couldn't he shake the lingering resentment?

"Would you like more shrimp?" she asked, passing him the plate of bacon-wrapped shrimp she'd grilled on the hibachi.

"Sure." He took it, and then eyed her plate. She'd

taken only two shrimp to start with, and granted they were huge suckers, but she still had one left. "Maybe not."

"You don't like it? Too much garlic?"

"I like it, all right." He shot a deliberate look at her plate. "I don't know if I trust them."

Her brows drew together for a moment, and then she grinned. "If I wanted to poison you, I'd be much more creative than that."

"Good. I wouldn't want to be such an easy mark." He forked a couple of shrimp, relieved to have dispelled the mild tension. "Considering how much garlic you used, in self-defense, you'd better have a couple more, too."

She took a nibble, and stared off toward the pink-and-orange-streaked horizon, the sun already disappearing. "I did get carried away, didn't I?"

"Everything okay back at the ranch?"

She looked blankly at him.

"The phone call you got earlier. You've seemed preoccupied since then."

"Oh." Immediately her expression turned guarded, and she couldn't have shut him out better if she'd raised a brick wall between them. "No big deal. It'll be okay. Want more pasta or salad?"

"Thanks, I'm good." He tried like hell not to take the rebuff personally. But, it wasn't as if he were prying. Just trying to make conversation.

She poured herself another glass of wine and then gestured toward his empty glass. He accepted the offer, determined to relax and enjoy the sunset.

After refilling his glass, Victoria sighed and picked up a shrimp with her fingers and then leaned back in her chair, nibbling her food and absently staring off toward the sinking sun. "I don't remember ever seeing the sky a more beautiful color."

"We have some pretty amazing sunsets in Houston, too."

"You're right. When I was a kid I used to sit in the garden and watch the sun set sometimes. I loved it when the black rain clouds would roll in off the bay and the pinks and oranges would look all the more vivid."

"You don't watch sunsets anymore?"

She shook her head. "Sad, isn't it? Seems like I'm always too busy."

"Not me. Never too busy for a sunset or a sunrise."

She gave him a curious look. "You spoke of a secretary earlier..."

"Selma. She slaps me upside the head when I need it."

"You haven't told me exactly what you do."

"Landscaping."

"You work for someone?"

"Nope. I have my own company. It's small. Only thirty full-time employees, and a dozen part-timers who work when they need the money or we have a big job. I like to get my hands dirty every once in a while, too."

"That's terrific. Do you do residential or commercial work?"

"Both."

"I assume you like the work."

"I wouldn't be doing it if I didn't."

She blinked, and looked away, but not before he saw the wistfulness in her eyes. It turned his stomach. "I'm glad you've found your calling and didn't follow in your dad's footsteps because it was easy."

"Is that what you did?"

Her entire body tensed, and her chin lifted. Her lips parted but she hesitated, as if mentally debating her reply. Finally she said, "Probably."

He waited anxiously for her to expand, not wanting to push her but hoping she'd feel comfortable enough to confide in him. The silence lengthened. Disappointed, he forced his gaze toward the open sea.

"I wish I had more contact with people," she finally said. "Of course I'm probably being premature. I need to learn more about the company before I'm assigned a position." She glanced briefly at him. "Which could end up being in promotion or sales."

"You don't know yet?" The words were barely out of his mouth and he cursed himself.

At the censure in his voice, she tensed again. "I haven't given it much thought. I'm sure my father will— Look, I really don't want to talk about work. This will probably be my only vacation this year."

"What?" He dropped his fork, letting it clatter to the plate.

She looked sharply at him.

He winked. "Don't forget. We have a date with Disneyland."

A smile slowly curved her lips. "I haven't forgotten," she whispered, wrapping her arms around herself, suddenly looking like the little girl who used to stand at the window all those years ago. "I might even hold you to it."

"THIS IS SEEMING LESS and less like a good idea."

"Chicken."

"You're damn right, and if you had any sense you would be, too."

Chuckling, Jake dropped his towel in the sand. "Come on, Victoria, where's your sense of adventure?"

She stood at the water's edge, wishing the moon wasn't quite so full. "Someone could walk by and see us. It's not like the beach has been deserted."

"No one's going to be walking around this late at night."

"We are."

"No, we're going skinny-dipping."

"I think not."

"Come on."

Tori shook her head. "I've changed my mind."

"Okay." Jake shoved off his shorts and threw them somewhere near his towel. "But I sure wish you'd join me." He stopped briefly to kiss her, a soft coaxing kiss that really got to her.

She watched him walk into the water, and then glanced around. In the distance, she saw muted light coming from the direction of their nearest neighbor, but other than that, not a soul in sight.

Jake had even turned off most of their lights. The deck was dark and only a light in the kitchen burned. A soft glow came from the bedroom, courtesy of the unusual shell night-light at the baseboard near the bathroom door.

God, she loved that house. Everything about it, from the sprawling rooms that blended into each other, to the quirky décor of beanbag chairs and tree stump end tables to the fish netting and shells on the walls.

"Victoria," Jake called out, drawing her attention back to him. "The water is mighty fine."

If there were a perfect night to go skinny-dipping, this was it. Dark enough that it took her a few seconds to locate him, and deserted enough that just maybe they wouldn't get arrested.

She sighed. Okay, she was overreacting. The Galveston police surely had better things to do than arrest people for skinny-dipping. But that didn't mean some little snippet wouldn't make it to the *Houston Chronicle* about Harrison Whitford's daughter being cited for lewdness.

She shuddered at the thought.

"Come on, Victoria."

She laughed at the childlike impatience in his voice, and then cupped her hands around her mouth to counter the breeze that had picked up, and called, "Make me an offer."

"What?"

"Give me a reason to join you."

He moved closer to shore until the water hit him waist-level. "What? I can't hear you."

She cupped her mouth again and hollered. "I said, what do I get if I—" Too late she realized what he was up to. He dashed out of the water easily covering ground over the hard-packed sand while she stumbled and lost her footing.

He caught her around the waist as she tried to right herself. "You want me to make you an offer, huh?" And then he picked her up, kicking and laughing, and carried her to the ocean.

# 12

"WHAT'S A THREE-LETTER WORD for a Tolkien tree creature?"

Jake took a bite out of his Asiago cheese bagel slathered with cream cheese and chewed thoughtfully as he watched Victoria frown at the Sunday *Chronicle*'s crossword puzzle. He'd never seen anyone look so serious over a damn crossword.

"Wait, let's look at twenty-six down first. That should help."

"Ent."

She looked up. "What?"

"A Tolkien tree creature is an ent."

Grinning, she went back to studying the puzzle.

"You don't believe me?"

Slowly she looked back up at him. "You're serious? You know that?"

"Yeah."

"How?"

"I don't know." He shrugged. "Probably from doing crosswords."

"I'm sorry. I didn't mean to hog this. I had no idea you liked to do puzzles."

"I don't anymore. I used to do them when I was bored in school." He smiled. "Anyway, I'd much rather watch you."

She looked down at herself sitting on the bed, wearing a too-big T-shirt that had slid off her left shoulder, one leg tucked under her, the other stretched wide, a tangle of sheets strategically bunched between her thighs. The newspaper was spread out over half the bed, the untouched bagel he'd toasted and buttered for her sitting on a plate in the middle of the front page.

She laughed. "I'm a mess."

"But very cute." Jake set his plate on the dresser and crawled in behind her. He only had on a pair of shorts, which he'd pulled on to go get the paper earlier. Sliding his arms around her waist, he pulled her back against his chest and rested his chin on her bare shoulder.

Relaxing against him, she made a soft noise of contentment. "So, you're going to help me with this?"

"No, I'm going to nibble your earlobe while you figure it out."

"And how am I supposed to concentrate?"

"That's your problem." He lightly bit the skin below her ear.

"Think so?" She threw down the pencil as if it were a gauntlet and straightened, preparing for battle.

"Careful—"

A second before she would've smashed her

bagel, he grabbed the plate and set it on the night-stand. She took advantage of the distraction, and clutching his shoulders, forced him to lie flat on his back. With a triumphant curve of her lips, she threw a leg over his waist and straddled him, keeping him pinned down.

He chuckled. "Am I supposed to protest?"

"Scream all you want. No one will hear you." She tried to keep a straight face, but failed miserably.

"Oh, yeah?" He worked a hand under her thigh. She jumped. "Hey."

"Sweetheart, you started it."

Laughing, she slid her hand under the waistband of his shorts, and struck gold. "Oh, my, what have we here?"

He groaned. "Keep that up and you can forget about the crossword."

She grinned at the pun and asked, "What cross-word?" Then she moved quickly and pulled his shorts off before he could defend himself.

Not that he would have. Naked was okay with him. As long as she joined him. He grabbed the hem of her T-shirt and she yelped and giggled at the same time, until she started coughing and gasping for breath.

"Take it easy." He immediately let go. "You okay?"

With a taunting laugh, she rolled out of reach.

"You fake."

"I outsmarted you." She stood, her shin lifted. "Don't be a poor sport."

He lunged for her, just as she started to walk away,

grabbing hold of the T-shirt again. She struggled to get away until the sound of the shirt tearing stopped her.

"Jake!"

"So what, it's mine." He fisted the stretchy fabric and pulled her backward until the back of her legs hit the bed.

"Damn it. You're gonna get it." She tumbled backward onto the mattress.

"I'm counting on it." This time he straddled her until he was able to get the shirt completely off, and they were both naked.

She stared up at him, her hazel eyes dancing with excitement and mischief. "You play dirty."

"Want me to stop?"

"Don't you dare." She slid a palm behind his neck and forced his mouth down to hers.

He kept the kiss gentle, teasing, seductive, hoping she'd become impatient and make another move. But the tables turned and he moved to her breast and tongued the beaded nipple before taking it into his mouth and suckling her until she moaned and her back arched off the mattress.

None too gently she reached for him, and grabbing hold began a firm, rhythmic stroke. He was already hard. Too hard. Especially considering they'd made love less than an hour ago.

They had only a day and a half left, and he wanted to go slow, make the most of every minute. He hoped he could talk her into staying longer, and he got the feeling she just might be agreeable.

"Easy, baby," he whispered, cupping his hand over hers.

She abruptly stopped. "Am I hurting you?"

"God, no." He grunted. "Just trying to slow things down, that's all."

"Oh." She smiled and resumed the rhythm that would soon be his undoing.

"You little devil," he murmured and distracted her with a well-placed finger.

She started, and then moaned softly.

The distinct sound of her cell phone playing *Fur Elise* penetrated the mood. She stiffened and met his eyes. He couldn't believe she'd even think about answering it now, but that's exactly what her eyes said.

"Let it go, Victoria." He probed with his finger, ran his tongue around the shell of her ear. "Whoever it is will leave a message."

"I can't." She pushed his hand away. "I'm sorry. I have to get it."

He watched her hurry to the phone where she'd left it out, lying beside her purse on the dresser, as if she'd expected to get a call. Damn, he hoped she missed it.

For crying out loud it was a Sunday morning. It couldn't be work. Hell, she'd said she was still studying up on the company. She didn't have any specific responsibilities yet. Which meant the call was personal. One of her more *suitable* boyfriends, no doubt.

Shit, none of his business.

Anger simmering in his gut, he heard her answer

with a soft "hello" and then watched her take the phone and slip into the bathroom. She closed the door without sparing him a look.

"WANT TO GO FOR A SWIM?"

"Maybe later." He concentrated on the sports section, even though he'd already read all the interesting articles. Checked the preseason injured list of the Cowboys, skimmed their stats twice. Better than letting her see how annoyed he was.

Victoria closed the sliding door behind her as she joined him on the deck. "I know you're still mad and I don't blame you." She moved in behind him and bending down, slid her arms around his neck, bringing her mouth close to his ear. "Can we call another truce?"

He wrapped a hand around her forearm and squeezed gently. "Question."

"Yes?" She tensed, but he tugged her arm and prompted her to swing around and sit on the chair beside him.

"You said you didn't blame me for being mad," he said, watching the green flecks flame in her guarded eyes. "Why?"

"Because if you'd suddenly jumped up in the middle of what we were doing to answer your cell phone, I would've been hurt and angry."

Unprepared for the blunt honesty, words momentarily escaped him.

Sighing, she took his hand. "The call wasn't about work. It wasn't even personal. Not really."

She exhaled sharply, as if struggling for an explanation. "It had something to do with the volunteer work I do. I really can't tell you much more than that—"

".You don't have to tell me anything."

"True." She smiled. "But I want you to know the call was really important or I wouldn't have taken it."

"Good enough."

"Really?"

Jake nodded. "I shouldn't have gotten irritated. We don't owe each other anything. Not even an explanation."

The wounded look on her face got to him. He hadn't meant to hurt her, but hell, she was the one who'd made the rules.

"Right." Her lips curved, but it wasn't a real smile she gave him.

"Look, Victoria, I didn't mean to—"

She held up a hand. "You're absolutely right. You don't need to say anything."

He grunted. Since when did being right feel so bad? "Want to go for that walk now?"

"Sure." She started to leave but he took her hand and pulled her toward him.

"Not so fast."

Without hesitation, she made herself comfortable on his lap and looped her arms around his neck. "What did you have in mind?"

He didn't speak. He showed her, by slipping his tongue between her lips and kissing her until she whimpered.

JAKE SHOOK OUT THE QUILT on a sparse patch of grass far enough from the water that they didn't have to worry about the tide. He set down the small cooler to anchor one end, and Victoria plopped down on the other.

She grinned up at him. "You think it's silly to drag our dinner out here, don't you?"

"I didn't say that."

"No, you didn't, and I appreciate you being a good sport."

"Anything to make you happy, darlin'."

She looked up at him with shining eyes and her lips curved in a smile he hadn't seen before. Kind of shy, but definitely happy. "I'm having the best time, Jake," she whispered. "The absolute best."

"Good." He sat beside her, slid an arm around her shoulders and pulled her close. "Me, too."

"I mean it."

"So do I." He kissed the side of her temple. Her hair smelled so sweet. Reminded him of vanilla.

"Jake?"

"Hmm?"

"Do you think we can come out here again?"

His heart thudded. "If you'd like," he said slowly, his thoughts beginning to race.

"Just for like a weekend or something, and I'd be happy to rent the house from your friends."

"That won't be necessary." He'd just bought the place. Signed the papers last month. Now was probably a good time to tell her.

Earlier he'd figured it was better not to mention

it in case she got weird and thought it was too personal to stay in a house he owned. But something had shifted in their relationship in the past couple of days. Nothing he could put a finger on, but she seemed more relaxed and open to talk of the future. Being together didn't seem so much about sex anymore.

Hell, maybe she could help him decorate, choose some furniture. The thought made his heart pump faster, his brain race with possibilities.

"I don't want you paying for it." She pulled back to look at him. "If anything we can split the cost."

It took him a couple of seconds to remember what she was talking about. "We don't need to rent the place. All we have to do is decide when we can take some time off. Once my father is back on his feet, I'll be more flexible."

She covered her mouth with her hand.

His heart sunk, certain she'd thought of a reason why she could never return. "What?"

"I feel horrible. I haven't even asked about your dad."

Jake sighed. "He's fine. I left his refrigerator fully stocked and the truck keys with Hector, who's also looking in on him until I get back." He laughed, fondly remembering his father slyly trying to get him to leave the truck keys. "He's ornery, but fine. Just needs to chill out and give himself time to heal."

"I haven't seen him for a really long time."

"His birthday is next weekend. I'll either take

him out to dinner or if he doesn't want to go out, have a small barbecue. Want to come?"

She frowned. "Next weekend?"

He nodded, already knowing her answer. She had that nervous look in her face that said he was getting too close and personal. Foolishly he'd thought they'd gotten past that barrier.

"I'm sorry, but I have a dinner to attend. It's a benefit and I committed a long time ago." She picked at the hem of her shorts. "It's going to be really boring, but it's for a good cause."

"Going alone?"

She shook her head and started digging into the cooler for their dinner. "My parents bought a table for ten. They'll be attending, along with my sister and her husband."

"If you need company to help get you through the evening—"

"Oh, God, I wouldn't do that to you," she said quickly. "I swear it'll be a yawner."

A moment of awkward silence followed and he wished he hadn't tried to invite himself along. He'd known she wouldn't bite. But her rejection stung and he'd childishly wanted to make her squirm.

"If you end up having the barbecue, would it be at his place?" she asked finally easing the tension. "I could probably come over for a while before or after the benefit."

"Sure."

"I imagine he still lives in the cottage around the corner."

"Still there. Too stubborn to move."

"Why would he? It's a cute place. I loved what he did with the planter boxes. And oh, my God, the tree house he built. Of course it probably isn't there anymore, huh?"

"You've been to the house?"

"Not for, gosh, at least fifteen years. I'm sure it's changed."

"What were you doing there?"

She winced, looking oddly sheepish. "He said he'd never tell. Obviously he hasn't. Bless his heart." A smile tugged at her mouth as if she were reliving a fond memory. "I was about ten or so and angry with my mother for something or other. Probably the usual disagreement over piano practice or being sent away to school.

"Anyway, I packed a toothbrush, a hairbrush and a book, and took off down the driveway. I made it around the corner and your dad stopped and asked if I needed a ride. I tried to be brave and say no but he bribed me with homemade butterscotch ice cream. I climbed into that shiny red truck of his and he took me to your house."

Jake sat in total amazement. His dad must have just bought the truck. He was so damn proud of it. "Where was I?"

"It was a regular school day. I guess that's where you and your sister were."

"He never said a word."

She smiled as she got out plates and napkins.

"He promised he wouldn't tell anyone. He said it would be our secret."

"How did he talk you into going home?"

She shrugged. "I don't remember exactly. I know he didn't rush me. He showed me the tree house, the model car collection you'd put together. Math and science papers you'd gotten A's on."

"You've got to be kidding."

"I remember that distinctly because I thought how wonderful it would be to have my father so proud of me." She visibly swallowed and quickly looked away. "I think I forgot to bring crackers."

"Victoria?"

"Hmm?" She kept her attention focused on the cooler, although obviously not interested in the contents.

"Hey, you." He lifted her chin.

She shuttered her eyes. "Look, I don't know about you but I'm starving. Open the olives, will you?"

He wouldn't let her ignore him. They were too close to sharing something important. "I think we all have different perspectives of our parents that eventually change as we get older. I had no idea my dad felt that way about my grades. He was always pleased with my report cards and gave me pats on the back, but that he saved test papers and actually showed them to someone else blows me away."

Her gaze steady with his, she frowned slightly. "I'm sure that's true in most cases. Except my perspective of my parents hasn't changed. I still think they're two self-absorbed people who shouldn't have had children."

He didn't know what to say to that. Hell, she was probably right.

"I'm not wallowing in self-pity," she added quickly. "It's a simple fact I've accepted." She made a face. "My only regret is that for a long time I avoided your dad. I was scared to death he'd tell my mother I'd run away." She smiled wryly. "She didn't even realize I'd been gone for more than half a day. Can you imagine a mother not knowing her ten-year-old child was missing?"

"No, I can't." He gave her hand a squeeze. "And don't pretend it doesn't hurt. You may be resigned intellectually, but that kind of stuff stays with you. I'm glad you're talking about it."

She stared down at the quilt and shrugged. "Mallory's in the same boat," she murmured. "It's not like woe-is-me." Her head abruptly came up. "I'm such a jerk. Complaining about my mother when you've never had one. I know she died when you were young."

"I was four. But don't worry about it. I don't even remember her, only what my father and grandparents told Sally and me about her. Dad has always been there for us so I honestly never felt deprived."

"You're lucky. He really is a terrific father."

"I know." He leaned over and kissed her gently.

She kissed him back harder, hungrier, but then stopped just as quickly and sat back. "We'd better eat before it gets too dark."

He nodded, knowing that she'd said all that she

wanted to say for now. Little by little her reserve was chipping away. If he didn't push and let things unfold naturally, maybe she'd be willing to stay a few more days. Maybe he'd learn more about her.

They finished unloading the cooler in silence. He smiled at the assortment of cheese and fruit, the two chocolate truffles she'd carefully packaged to keep from crushing. He was getting a clear picture of her favorite foods.

"Next time we go to the market, let's pick up a summer sausage before I turn into a damn rabbit."

She glanced at the spread and laughed at his playful grumbling. "Point taken. Although I doubt cheese is part of a rabbit's diet."

"Don't get technical." Pleased that she hadn't reacted negatively to mention of another market trip, he dug into a piece of Gouda, his hope renewed.

Later, while they were in bed, he'd bring up the possibility of staying until next Thursday. Why not make it an even week? Or better yet, stay through next weekend. Who ever heard of returning to work on a Friday?

He opened a bottle of Evian for each of them, and then helped himself to a handful of strawberries. He started to tease her about sharing the truffles when her cell phone rang. He didn't know she had it with her. Although he should have figured.

With a brief look of apology, she unhooked the phone from her waistband and answered it.

"No bother, Kathryn," she replied to the caller. Indecision flashed in her eyes, and then she slowly got to her feet.

It didn't surprise him that she'd want to talk in privacy. He reminded himself it wasn't personal as she walked toward the water. A second before she got out of earshot he heard her say, "I'll be there tomorrow morning."

That, he took personally.

# 13

TORI RUSHED INTO Kathryn's office, belatedly realizing she hadn't even knocked. "Sorry for interrupting," she murmured. "Please tell me Beth is still here."

The older woman stopped writing and studied her pensively for a second. "She's still here. I believe she's upstairs reading to the children."

"Thank God. If she'd gone back to the scumbag last night, I never would have forgiven myself."

Kathryn laid down her pen. "Tori, we need to talk."

She sighed, fully prepared for the lecture. "I know what you're going to say. But may I please see Beth first?"

"No, you're going to sit down and listen."

Tori did as she was told, totally unprepared for the sternness in Kathryn's voice.

The older woman's expression gentled. "Look, I know you mean well, but you can't drop your life to live Beth's."

Tori reared her head back at the absurdity of the statement. "That's pretty strong."

"Good. Then it should sink in well. Tori, you're a great asset to this center. You're caring and supportive and reliable. But if you keep getting emotionally involved, you're gonna burn out."

"Let me worry about that."

"That's not my main concern. You'll continue to cripple the Beths of the world. These women have to learn how to stand up for themselves." Kathryn sighed and shook her head. "I can't tell you how many times I've wanted to kick myself for calling you to talk to Beth that day. I was being foolish and impulsive."

"No, you weren't. I told you when I started here I was in wholeheartedly."

Kathryn smiled sadly. "That's the problem. I should've known you weren't capable of emotionally detaching yet. It was too soon to involve you on a personal level with any of the women. See? After all these years of seasoning, even I panicked and made a wrong call."

"You didn't. It's not as if I cut my vacation short," Tori said, with a twinge of guilt, remembering the disappointment on Jake's face when she told him she had to get back to Houston. "Or had to jump on a plane to get here. I'd spent a few days in Galveston. That's all."

Thoughtfully, Kathryn pursed her lips. "It's real easy to focus on someone else's problems so that you don't have to deal with your own."

Tori's mouth fell open.

Kathryn held up a hand. "I'm not saying that's the case with you. Only you can be the judge of that. I'm just warning you to be careful. We're all vulnerable here, Tori. We forget that for one minute and we're in trouble."

Feeling horribly fragile and exposed suddenly, Tori took a deep breath. "This sounds more personal. If you have a point to make about me, go ahead. I'm a big girl. I can take it."

Kathryn stared back, the indecision in her eyes clear. She smiled wanly. "You've made a couple of remarks that indicate you're unhappy with your job. I'm wondering if this isn't a substitute, that maybe you feel trapped. Have you thought about a career change? You're awfully good at this and—

"That's ridiculous. My job is new and learning the ropes is frustrating. That's all."

"Fine. You know best." Kathryn picked up her pen again. "Like we tell the women. It's not about quitting but about being smart and knowing when to cut your losses. Learning to put yourself first. Putting aside our fear of failure because if we don't try, we automatically fail." With a sly smile, she added. "But you know all that. I don't have to tell you."

The air in the office seemed thin all of a sudden. Tired from lack of sleep, Tori wanted to get home and crawl into bed. Of course she'd talk to Beth first so she'd know that Tori had kept her word. She would always be here if Beth needed her, and she wouldn't have to live in fear that someone could take her children from her.

That didn't diminish anything Kathryn had warned against. What she'd said made sense. Fortunately it didn't apply to Tori. She certainly wasn't trying to escape her own problems. Nor was she fearful of change. She had the security of a career, money, a good education and a promising future. She had it all.

At least, everyone seemed to think so.

"MOST PEOPLE TAKE vacations to relax and rejuvenate, and when they come back to work they're full of energy and renewed enthusiasm."

Jake looked up from his desk to see Selma standing in the doorway of his office, one hand on her hip. "I was gone for a lousy four days. That's hardly a vacation."

"Don't argue semantics." She entered and sat in the chair opposite him. "Are you going to tell me why you've been sulking for the past two days?"

"No."

"Then will you stop it?"

"I'm not sulking. I'm busy."

Her gaze went to the stack of invoices he hadn't touched for the past two hours. "Jake, you haven't been yourself for over two weeks now. Whatever is bothering you, I hope you have someone to talk to."

If not for the concern in her eyes, he would've told her to butt out. "Honest, I'm fine. The Forever Green deal has me edgy. That's all."

"Well, after you meet with the attorneys today and go over the contract, maybe you'll feel better."

"Today?" His gaze flew to his calendar, and then to his watch. "Son of a bitch."

Selma wisely stayed silent. After a moment she rose and headed for the door. "You still have a couple of hours. Let me know if you need anything."

Hell, what he needed was his head examined. He'd been too damn busy trying to decide whether he should call Victoria or not. Or wondering why she hadn't called him. Their last night hadn't been spent talking, and then they'd kind of left things up in the air once they got to Houston.

All he knew was that she'd been preoccupied with the phone call she'd received the night before they left Galveston. She hadn't offered an explanation, and he hadn't asked.

Hell, maybe it was something serious that was keeping her involved. They hadn't even been back for forty-eight hours. No use obsessing. He couldn't afford the distraction. After having agreed to move up the contract meeting with the attorneys, he had too much going on.

Once he signed on the dotted line and turned over this latest patent, he could take off as much time as he wanted. Go buy a cabin cruiser like he'd seen at the beach. Maybe talk Victoria into breaking in the boat and taking a run with him to San Padre Island for another long weekend.

No matter where his thoughts headed, they always ended up with her.

He pushed away from his desk and went to check behind his door for the shirt and khakis he kept on a hook for days like today when he forgot he had a meeting to attend. The fact that he needed to keep spare clothes was evidence enough that he didn't care for the business end of the job.

He liked it best when he got an idea for a way to simplify a landscaping task and could tinker in his garage until he made the idea work. So far, his designs had paid off with two successful patents, and lucrative interest from Forever Green.

The slacks weren't too wrinkled and the shirt had recently been returned from the cleaners. He was about to close his office door so he could change clothes when a thought occurred to him.

"Hey, Selma." He poked his head into the outer office. "There is something you can do for me. Remember that invitation to the Safe Haven Center benefit dinner?"

She nodded.

"Wasn't the dinner for this Saturday?"

"I can't remember. But you told me to send a check and a regret."

He rubbed the back of his neck, hoping this was the right benefit. As a small business owner he got a ton of solicitations for various Houston charities. "I've changed my mind. Call somebody and get me a ticket, would you? Oh, and find a place where I can rent a tux."

Selma's jaw dropped.

He sighed and closed his office door before she could ask him why he was being such an idiot.

TORI PINCHED THE BRIDGE of her nose. She was tired of reading reports that meant nothing to her. Tired of worrying about Beth. Tired of wondering if Jake would call. Ridiculous, because of course she could call him. And it looked as if she were going to have to if she wanted to see him.

God, she hoped he wasn't still angry about having to return a day early. No, he hadn't been angry. Disappointed. Which was far worse, in her opinion.

She eyed the phone. Maybe she should call now and get it out of her system so she could get down to the business of finishing her reading. But then again, if she called now, and heard his voice, she wouldn't be able to concentrate for the rest of the afternoon.

"Victoria?"

"Hi, Dad." She smiled up at her father. "Come in."

He hovered at her office door, glancing at his watch, his eyebrows pulled together in a frown. "I have five minutes before I have to meet with Simon Schmidt from the legal department. I thought perhaps you'd like to sit in on the meeting."

"Well, sure." She tried to look enthusiastic. "What's it about?"

"A potential lawsuit filed by one of our suppliers. Probably a nuisance suit but nevertheless it needs to be addressed." His gaze went to the reports sitting on her desk. He stepped closer, his frown deepening. "You haven't finished reviewing those yet?"

Heat crept into her cheeks. "I have," she said, hating to lie. Tonight for sure, she'd take everything home and read all the way through to the last page even if it took all night. "But there's so much information that I needed to revisit a few points."

He studied her for a moment, his expression unreadable. Her own father and she didn't have the vaguest clue as to what he was thinking. "I hadn't meant for you to fine-tooth comb everything. A general familiarization would have sufficed." He glanced again at his watch. "Look, forget about going to this meeting. I'm sure you're anxious to start assimilating into your new position. We'll talk about it when I'm done. In the meantime, finish up there."

"Wait." Tori's gaze flew to the clock on her desk. "What time would that be?"

Impatience flashed in his eyes. "Are you still volunteering at that place?"

"Yes," she said, lifting her chin. She should be flattered. Apparently her parents had found time to discuss her.

He frowned in thought. "We'll meet tomorrow then. Check with my secretary. I think I have half an hour open in the morning."

She nodded, and then leaned back and slowly exhaled after he disappeared. At least he hadn't made any disparaging remarks about her working at the center. That was something. And now she didn't have to read any more of these boring reports.

Except tomorrow was D Day. The thought filled her with so much dread she got a little queasy. Assignment of a position meant accountability and responsibility, neither of which would bother her if she had the slightest interest in the manufacturing of engine parts.

She'd even gone so far as to study the company's organizational chart trying to figure out where she could fit in to her liking. The only department remotely interesting was human resources. And that was out, unless she wanted to negotiate with the unions or mediate grievances or coordinate benefits with insurance companies. Other than that, what employee would want to discuss anything with the boss's daughter?

Sighing, she briefly closed her eyes and thought about Jake, the beach house, Galveston... She wished they were still there, sitting on the deck soaking up the sun, laughing, talking, kissing...

She opened her eyes and stared at the phone. It wasn't her fault her father had assumed she was scheduled to work at the center tonight. As it happened, she had a free evening. And she'd be damned if she'd wait around for Jake to call.

After getting up and closing her office door, she dialed his cell number. And got his voice mail. Muttering a curse, she was about to hang up. She stopped, thought for a second and then left a message instead.

The ball was in his court.

JAKE PULLED INTO THE HOTEL parking lot half an hour late. He hoped Victoria was still there. He'd tried to call her back after his marathon meeting with the attorneys, but he got her voice mail twice.

He skipped the front desk and went straight to the room they'd used the last two times. The second he knocked he realized how stupid it was to assume she'd gotten this room.

She opened the door and smiled.

His heart thumped. Had it really been only two days since he'd seen her?

"Hi." She stepped back, opening the door wider.

"Hi back at you."

"I'm glad you came."

"Of course I'd come." He closed the door behind him. "I was in a meeting when you called. I only picked up the message an hour ago."

"Oh, yeah." She looked down at his khakis. "You've got your grown-up clothes on."

Chuckling, he grabbed her hand and pulled her toward him. She came willingly, and breathlessly met his lips. She tasted so damn good. Felt good, too, as he ran his hands down her back over her firm round backside.

His body had started to react as soon as he'd gotten off the elevator, but it was different this time. He wasn't so anxious to get down to business. Holding her like this felt too damn good.

"I've missed you," she whispered against his mouth.

He pulled back and brushed the hair away from her face. "Me, too."

"And the beach. I miss the water."

"I'm glad I topped the list."

She laughed softly. "That was an oversight. We need to keep your ego in check."

"I think it's been behaving." He slid his arms around her and pulled her close, enjoying her soft sigh of contentment. "You get everything taken care of?"

She stiffened slightly. "What do you mean?"

"The reason we came back early."

"Oh, that." She lifted a shoulder. "Sort of. The problem hasn't gone away, but I think we were able to cheat the Grim Reaper one more time."

"Whoa, I don't like the sound of that."

"I was just being whimsical." She groaned and straightened to look at him, the sparkle gone from her eyes. "But those golden days of whimsy are about to end."

"Bad news?"

She made a sound of disgust.

He smiled. "Let's go sit down."

She let him lead her to the edge of the bed, and he positioned himself against the headboard, legs spread, so that he could pull her against him. Pressing her cheek to his chest, she snuggled in the circle of his arms.

"Tell me about it," he said, resting his chin atop her head.

"Tomorrow is the big day with my father. He's gonna lower the boom." She giggled. "That's a funny expression, isn't it? I haven't heard it in ages. I don't even know where it came from."

"Don't procrastinate."

"I'm not. But I have to find humor in the situation or else go nuts. Tomorrow morning we discuss my role in the business."

"And?"

"What do you mean, and?" She brought her head up, her tone obviously annoyed.

He coaxed her back into a relaxed position. "You knew this was coming. It's not a surprise."

"Don't get rational on me."

"Sorry."

She heaved a big sigh. "I can't talk to him tomorrow. I don't know what I want to be when I grow up."

"Poor baby." Grinning at her exaggerated whininess, he stroked her hair. "Take another week. Tell him you're not ready to decide yet."

"It's not a matter of what I decide. It's what my father thinks is best for the company."

"He's not going to push you in a direction you don't want to go."

She didn't say anything.

"Victoria?"

She groaned. "Let's not talk about it anymore. It'll just ruin my night."

"All right, but promise me something."

"What's that?" She sat up straight and pressed her palm against his chest, using her thumb to play with his nipple through his shirt.

He sucked in a breath. "Don't let your father intimidate you into a position you don't want."

"It's not a matter of wanting or not wanting. He'll put me where I can do the most good for the company."

"And that can only be a position you enjoy. If you hate your job, you won't be effective."

"I don't need a lecture from you, thank you very

much." She got off the bed and moved away before he could stop her.

"I'm *not* lecturing."

"Look, you don't understand. It's complicated. It's a family thing."

"Then make it a Victoria thing." He got up and followed her to the bathroom, taking hold of her hand before she closed the door. "Make it about you. Make it personal. Take control. You're the one who has to live the consequences. Not your father, or anyone else."

She faced him, her eyes slowly narrowing. "Why?"

"Because your career is a big chunk of your life. It can effect your total outlook on—"

"No." Obviously frustrated, she shook her head. "Why are you telling me this? Why do you care?"

He released her hand. "Oh yeah, sorry. I forgot I'm not supposed to care about you."

"Jake, come on. That's not what I meant."

"Go to the bathroom." Shoving a hand through his hair, he started back toward the bed.

"I don't have to."

"You did a second ago."

She touched his shoulder to get his attention. "I was afraid I might tear up and I didn't want you to see that."

He looked into her earnest eyes, a lump forming in his throat. He couldn't remember ever seeing her look so vulnerable. "Why would you tear up?"

"Because..." She moistened her lips. "Because I know you do care."

"And that's a problem?"

She blinked a couple of times and then slid her arms around him. "Hold me."

He did as she asked, gathering her close, wishing like hell he could see her face. But she held on tight, rocking gently to a silent beat.

Their meeting tonight sure as hell wasn't about sex and he wondered if she realized that.

# 14

TORI'S CELL RANG while she was stuffing envelopes and manning the center's hot line. She checked caller ID before answering and smiled.

Jake responded to her hello by asking, "How did it go?"

"I had a stay of execution."

"He canceled your meeting?"

"Yep. He had to go out of town."

"See that? You were worried for nothing."

She sighed. "It's not as if he's going to be gone for long. He only went to San Francisco. He's returning this weekend."

"Ever been there?"

"San Francisco?"

"Yeah."

"Twice."

"What did you think?"

"Both times it was too cold and foggy to see anything." Tori leaned back in the rickety office chair, forgetting how unstable it was and nearly fell. She gasped as she grabbed the lip of the desk.

"Victoria? What's wrong?"

She laughed. "Nothing, really. I'm sitting in this old relic and I tilted too far back."

"Where are you?"

She hesitated. Oh, brother. She'd already complained to him about her job and her mother. What did it matter if he knew that she volunteered? "At the place I volunteer."

"Ah." He sounded surprised. "I was just going to ask you to go for a drink. I guess that's out, huh?"

She looked at her watch. It was already Thursday and she hadn't found a dress for Saturday night yet. "I can't. I have to stay here for another two hours, and then I have an errand to run."

"No problem. I figured if the boom had been lowered, you might want to drown your sorrows."

She laughed. "Where are you?"

"Still at the office."

"So late?"

His deep chuckle sent a delicious shiver down her spine. "Selma is busting my balls over what she calls dereliction of duty. I swear I'm gonna set her up with my father so she has another hobby besides me."

Tori grinned. "I don't know her but I like her."

"You would."

"Hey, what did you decide to do for your dad for his birthday?"

"No barbecue. He hated the idea."

"Is he touchy about his age?"

"Nah. He's not big on celebrating anything besides Christmas. And even that is done grudgingly and for the sake of the grandkid."

She twirled the phone cord around her fingers and let her thoughts drift back to last night. They hadn't done anything more than cuddle and the warm fuzzy feeling still hadn't left her. "When's your birthday?"

"Why?"

"I want to know what sign you are."

"Aries."

"Come on, just tell me when it is."

He chuckled. "March 28. Why did you want to know?"

"That's not for another six months." Tori loved celebrating birthdays. At boarding school they always had festive parties for the girls' birthdays with decorations and games and prizes. It was the best thing about being away at school. Birthdays at home meant dinner at the Club. Sometimes her father would even show up.

"Hey, don't rush things. I just hit the big 'three-o.' When's your birthday?"

"Why?"

"You give me the third degree and you have the nerve to ask why?"

She grinned. "Next month."

"October? What does that make you?"

"A libra, of course."

He chuckled. "Of course. Sounds like you take these signs seriously."

"No, except I'm very much a libra in every way."

"Aren't libras supposed to be rational people?"

"Screw you."

He let out a deep throaty laugh that made her tingle. "I thought you'd never ask."

"You're awful."

"One of the many things you love about me, right?"

Tori blinked, a funny feeling starting to churn in her stomach. He'd used a figure of speech, of course. They both knew love wasn't part of their equation. "I'm gonna have to be shoving off here. I have a lot of things to do before my shift ends."

"Then tonight's definitely out?"

Oh, God, she was tempted... "I'm afraid so."

"No problem. Maybe tomorrow night."

"I'll call you." She wouldn't see him tomorrow night. They needed some space. But she couldn't bring herself to tell him yet.

"You have my number."

"Yeah."

"Victoria?"

"Yes." Something in his tone made her entire body tense in anticipation of what he was going to say.

"About your birthday. What do you say we take that trip to Disneyland to celebrate?"

She bit her lower lip. What the hell had she done? She forced a laugh that came out shaky. "That's a month and a half away yet."

"Just wanted to give you something to think about."

"Okay." She didn't know what else to say. This was her fault. She'd gotten too close. Shared too many confidences. She'd broken her own rules. And now she didn't know what the hell to do about it.

"WHAT ABOUT THIS ONE?" Mallory held up a green cocktail dress. "I don't think you've worn it yet."

Sitting near her bedroom closet with a Coke and a bag of chips, Tori frowned at the strapless silk sheath. "I'm not sure I can fit into it."

Her sister laughed and plucked a tortilla chip out of Tori's hand. "Maybe if you'd stop stuffing your face with these things you'd be able to get into it."

Tori glared at her. "I'm going to show incredible restraint here and not say a word."

"Go ahead. Complain about my drinking." Mallory shrugged and took another sip of her martini. "Everyone else does."

Tori swallowed, and took a deep breath. "If everyone has mentioned it, don't you think it might be something to think about?"

"Oh, sure, I think about it all the time." She wrinkled her nose. "Let's see, do I want an olive or an onion? Gin or vodka?"

"I'm serious, Mallory."

"I know...but this is a stressful time with the house being renovated and Richard away all the time. It's not as if I drink like this when I'm home alone."

Tori didn't believe that for a minute. And Mallory knew it judging by the way she quickly transferred her attention to another dress.

"What do you think of this one?" Mallory held out a turquoise sequined dress at arm's length.

"Definitely too froufrou."

"Then why did you buy it?"

"I didn't."

"Mother?"

Tori nodded.

"Ah."

They both laughed, and then Tori said, "Don't I have anything in there that's basic black?"

"Like you were going to a funeral?"

"Exactly."

Mallory made a face. "I thought you endorsed Safe Haven."

"I do. But I hate going to these black-tie affairs."

"Take a date. Then it might not be so boring." Mallory continued rummaging through Tori's closet, pulling out several more dresses, two of them black.

Tori sat back, leaning against the headboard of her bed and nibbled another chip. Jake would make the evening fun. Of course that was out of the question. She looked at her bedside clock. It was late. Too late to call and ask him to go have a drink. Which was a bad idea, anyway. Not just bad, but horrible, dangerous.

Nothing had changed since she'd talked to him earlier. In fact, she should be even more cautious. She couldn't let him talk about the future. There would be no trips to Disneyland or San Francisco together. She'd been treating the past few weeks like a vacation. That had to end very soon and then she wouldn't have time to see him at all.

The idea made her sick to her stomach and she pushed aside the bag of chips.

Yeah, the sex was great and no guy she knew had a better body, but that wasn't it. There was so much more about him she was going to miss. No one could make her laugh like Jake. Or make her think. The kind of deep, soul-searching reflecting that could be uncomfortable as hell, but like a shot in the arm, you knew it was good for you in the long run.

"I personally like this little blue ruffled number. How long have you had it? Twenty years?" Mallory looked at her and immediately stopped laughing. "What's wrong?"

"Nothing."

"You're as pale as a sheet."

"Probably too many chips and Coke."

Mallory's gaze narrowed. "You aren't pregnant, are you?"

"God, no. Are you crazy? How could I be pregnant?"

"I doubt I have to explain that process to you."

"You're right. You don't." Tori forced a laugh. "Let me see that black silk you laid over the chair."

Mallory picked up the dress, her brows still drawn together in a frown. "You probably ought to stay home from work tomorrow."

"I don't think I've accrued enough sick time yet."

Mallory snorted as she held up the dress for Tori. "This isn't bad. I think I'd go with this one."

Tori nodded. "Works for me."

"Better try it on."

"I will later."

Mallory set down the dress and sat next to Tori on the bed. "Are you sure you're okay?"

"No, but I will be."

"Anything you want to talk about?"

Tori pressed her lips together. She couldn't discuss Jake with her sister. Not that she didn't trust Mallory, but it was pointless. Jake didn't fit into her life's plan. She knew that, like she knew the sun would rise tomorrow, and no amount of whining or wishing would change that.

She looked into her sister's concerned eyes and smiled. "Really, I'm okay. Just tired as hell."

"Didn't get much rest on your vacation, huh?"

"It wasn't exactly a vacation," Tori muttered. "You know how those sorority reunions are. Late night gossiping and eating junk food."

"Hmm, I haven't been to one yet. Of course I haven't been out of school that long," she said pointedly, a grin tugging at her lips, making Tori want to throw a pillow at her.

So what if she suspected Tori had been lying about the weekend? As long as she kept her suspicions to herself it didn't matter.

"Well, I'd better go to my room and ravage my closet." Mallory got to her feet. "Richard is coming home tomorrow. Wonder if I'll recognize him."

Tori laughed. "How long has be been gone now?"

"I don't know. Four or five weeks."

"That's a long time. Why didn't you go with him?"

Mallory reared her head back, blinking in surprise, making Tori think the idea had never occurred to her sister. "He's working. I'd be bored silly."

"You're bored here."

Mallory laughed softly. "Good point."

A wild thought struck Tori. Since Mallory and Richard had been married, his lengthy absences were many. Sure, they were a result of work, but that still precluded him from many social obligations the rest of the family endured.

So if Jake was in her life, why should he be expected to suit up and show up? The idea had merit. She really had to think about this...

She silently cleared her throat, and casually asked, "Is Richard going to the benefit on Saturday?"

Mallory's lips curved in a sly smile. "I didn't tell him about it yet. Otherwise he probably would have waited until Monday to come home."

"You're bad."

"I try my best." She stopped near the door and bent to pick up a pair of Tori's strappy sandals. "I haven't seen these before. Very cute."

Her brain on overload, Tori just stared at her sister. So much had gone though her head in the past few minutes. Hope for both Jake and her sister. Mallory sounded so much like her old self. And Jake...well, why not Jake?

"Mall?"

"I wish we wore the same size," her sister murmured and then looked up. "What?"

"Come to work with me tomorrow."

Mallory dropped the sandals and frowned. "Are you crazy? Why would I do that?"

"It could be fun. It's time the company got a dose of the new generation of Whitfords."

"Fun? You must have a fever." She sighed. "I love you, Victoria. But honey, you forgot, I already gave at the office. They have Richard."

"I BELIEVE YOUR CELL PHONE is ringing, Victoria."

"I know. It's okay." Tori peered at the sandwich her secretary set on her desk. "What's this?"

"Turkey on whole wheat."

"No, I mean I told you not to bring me back anything."

"I know you did, but I made an executive decision." Karen folded her arms across her chest. "Now, eat."

Tori rolled her eyes. "Yeah, like I don't look like I could miss a few meals."

"You know that's the first time you've come close to smiling all day."

"That's a crime?"

"You're not generally sarcastic. Your eyes aren't usually so red. And you certainly don't spend the day working as hard as you have today."

"Ouch. Now that hurt."

"I'm not going to ask you what's wrong. It's none of my business. But I don't want you sick, either. Between you and your sister, next thing you know I won't have a job." She winked before turning to leave.

Tori sighed and yawned, her head still splitting after taking three aspirins. Thankfully the phone had stopped ringing. She'd checked caller ID on the first ring and knew it was Jake. He'd probably leave another message she'd eventually have to return. If she didn't think Beth might call, she would have turned the damn thing off.

She squinted at the notes she'd taken, her handwriting barely legible after having scribbled twenty-three pages of notes, questions she had for her father regarding the different departments.

Even though she was exhausted from no sleep last night, her determination to get a handle on the company hadn't wavered. She was in this for the long haul, no question, but equally important, her new resolve helped to keep her from thinking about Jake. From playing that last scene with Mallory last night, over and over again in her head.

Every Whitford contributed to the strength of the company and the Whitford name in some way, shape or form. That's the way it was. How could she have forgotten that for even a single second? Why should she be different? You either contributed personally or married well. Preferably both.

The sight of the turkey sandwich made her stomach roll and she shook out the napkin and laid it on top. It was far past lunchtime anyway. In fact, she was startled to realize how close to four it was already.

She had to return Jake's call. He didn't deserve her rudeness. Or her cowardice. She'd made a horrible mistake getting too close to him. Now it was up to her to break it off gently. He shouldn't be too upset. He knew all she'd ever wanted was sex.

She flinched at the thought. So much had changed. Jake wasn't just the gardener's son anymore. He was...Jake. Like it or not, they already had something more than sex.

Taking a deep shuddering breath she closed her eyes. Folding her arms, she rested them on her desk and laid her forehead on them.

God, this was *not* going to be easy.

JAKE PACKED IT UP for the evening, clearing his desk and locking up the sketches and files of his latest design. He looked at his watch: 6:47. Houston traffic never seemed to die down but maybe it wouldn't be so brutal by now. On Fridays people tended to get out of work early or at least on time.

Damn, he wished Victoria had called by now. He'd left two messages on her cell phone. That was it. He wouldn't leave another. If she wanted to call him, she would. Nothing to get uptight about. She'd probably been in a meeting this afternoon. Maybe her father had gotten back...

There was still some coffee in the pot and he poured it into his cup and nuked it in Selma's microwave. Normally he drank coffee black, but it was thick and dark and stale enough that he added some cream and sugar to make it more palatable before he took it back to his desk.

He sunk into his chair and yawned widely. If he'd had a brain in his head, he would have used last night to catch up on sleep. Not spend most of it tinkering in his garage. The thing was, when he'd tried to lie down, all he could think about was Victoria.

Man, he couldn't understand her. She was smart, strong and determined yet when it came to her family's dictates, she acted like a loyal follower. And her father...didn't he see she wasn't happy working for the company? Hell, a blind person could see that.

His cell phone rang and he nearly knocked the coffee over trying to grab it. He saw that it was her before he answered.

"Hey."

"Hey," she said back.

"I was hoping you'd call."

"Oh, sorry I didn't get back to you sooner. Busy day."

"I figured. You still at the office?"

"Not exactly," she murmured around a yawn and an apology. "I'm sitting in my car in the underground parking lot."

"Is that safe?"

"Yep. Tons of security. In fact, they're probably wondering what I'm doing here sitting in the dark."

He lowered his voice suggestively. "What are you doing?"

She laughed softly. "You're awful."

Smiling, hopeful that she'd be in the mood to see him tonight, he said, "I know what I'd like you to be doing."

She hesitated, and then with excitement in her voice, she whispered, "Tell me."

"Standing here in front of me, unbuttoning your blouse." He leaned back in his chair and closed his eyes. "Which bra are you wearing?"

"The red lacy one."

"Hmm, one of my favorites." He shifted to a more comfortable position, already too aroused for his own good. "I'd flip that clasp in the front and push the cups aside so I could see those two perfect breasts. Those perfect rosy-colored nipples that I can almost taste..."

She moaned. "Okay, I've heard enough."

"I'd push your blouse off your shoulders, throw it aside with the bra and then slide my arms around you, kissing and licking you, while I unzipped the back of your skirt."

"Okay, I get the picture," she said breathlessly. "It's getting mighty warm in here."

He chuckled. "I'm not through."

"Yes, you are." She sighed. "Jake, I have to go."

He stiffened. "You have plans tonight?"

"Unfortunately, yes."

*Shit.* He passed a hand over his face and then rubbed his jaw. He wouldn't ask where she was going. "Any chance I can see you later?"

"I'm afraid not."

"All right."

She made a soft sound of indecision. "It's my mother. She set me up on another one of those dates," she said breezily. "I swear I don't know why she's so anxious to marry me off."

"Ah." At a loss for words that wouldn't betray his anger, he said, "Have fun, Victoria." Then he hung up.

# 15

To: The Gang at Eve's Apple
From: Angel@EvesApple.com
Subject: The gutless wonder

I know I haven't written to you guys in a while. I've been way too busy being the biggest idiot in the world. Who should be shot at dawn. Except that would be too easy, and I don't deserve leniency.

Guys, I have screwed up royally. It's humiliating to admit how royally. I went away with J for the four days. (Actually, we had to cut it a little short but that's another story.) Anyway, the truth is, I would've stayed the whole week if I could have, hell, two weeks wouldn't have been enough.

He's the most wonderful man I've ever met. Funny, patient, smart, and the sex... I'll spare you by not going there. But trust me, he's everything a woman could want. He even likes kids.

<<Major sigh>> I totally blew it. I got too close. We read the Sunday paper in bed!!! I let him help with the crossword! (Help, hah. He got more words than I did). I have no idea what came over me.

Now, I've got to break it off. Stop things before the relationship gets any more complicated.

I'm trying to be brave and sensible and do the right thing by him. He deserves an easy letdown. Not like what I did last night. Told him I couldn't meet him because I had another date. See? I'm pond scum. I'm blowing things all the way around. I need HELP, guys. Desperately!!!
Love,
Angel, the big fat chicken


Tori hit Send and then closed her laptop and squinted at her bedside clock. Already 2:00 a.m. and she hadn't slept for a single minute. By tomorrow night she'd be a wreck if she didn't get some rest. She set her computer aside, turned off the light, then slid deep under the covers and prayed for mind-numbing sleep.


To: The Gang at Eve's Apple
From: Barbara@EvesApple.com
Subject: The gutless wonder
Angel,
The sex is that great and you're gonna spare us? Please!!!!! You should be shot at dawn.

Hate to sound dense but I don't get it. The guy is wonderful, funny, smart, patient... So what's the problem!?! Sounds like you lucked out, kiddo. I say don't hesitate, go full speed ahead.
Love and kisses,
Barbara

To: The Gang at Eve's Apple
From: Taylor@EvesApple.com
Subject: Make love, not war
Angel,

I'm with Barbara. He sounds perfect. Unless you're already engaged or something, I don't see a problem. I've got a confession to make. When I was first seeing Ben and wondering what I should do, you wrote an e-mail that bothered me. A very pessimistic e-mail about how true supreme happiness with the opposite sex is meant to be temporary. You said that life isn't a fairy tale but if I was really lucky I could be a princess for just a little while.

I didn't believe it then, or at least I didn't want to believe it, and I absolutely don't believe it now. I think that's the kind of stuff we all tell ourselves in case we don't meet Mr. Right. Don't believe your own propaganda, Angel. Two years, five, ten years from now you'll look back and say if only... Don't do that to yourself. Give yourself a chance. And J, too.

I'm thinking about you.

Love,
Taylor

Tori reread each e-mail and tried to stay calm. They were supposed to be her friends, her allies. None of this was helpful. It sounded as if they were on Jake's side.

Still exhausted after only three hours of sleep, she sighed and set the laptop aside. She was tired and overreacting. Of course she hadn't laid out the whole story for them so they didn't have a picture of her family situation. It wasn't fair to expect the gang to understand and sympathize.

She rolled out of bed and headed for the bathroom. A shower and shampoo would make her feel better. And if the circles under her eyes hadn't disappeared by this evening, she'd just have to slap on a ton of makeup.

Anyway, what did she care what she looked like tonight? The only person she wanted to impress wouldn't be at the benefit.

WHITE-GLOVED WAITERS passed silver trays artfully laden with canapés and flutes of champagne. Tables set with sparkling crystal and royal-blue china shone under dazzling chandeliers. On the stage, the band softly played "Moon River."

"So good to finally meet you." Marian Whitford shook Kathryn's hand. "The room looks marvelous. You've done a wonderful job with this year's benefit." She glanced around the ballroom. "In fact, I think this may be the best turnout in the past ten years. Don't you think, girls?" She smiled at Mallory and Tori.

They both nodded and smiled back, and then Mallory whispered, "She's so full of it. She only said that so Kathryn knows she's been a patron for that long."

Tori pressed her lips together to keep from laughing. Her sister was sounding more and more like her old self. Too much at times. "Keep your voice down," Tori whispered back. "Or it's going to be one hell of a long dinner."

"A lot of thanks goes to your daughter," Kathryn said, and Tori stiffened. "She's been invaluable to me for the past three weeks. Didn't hesitate for a second to jump in and roll up her sleeves."

Her mother gave Tori a tight smile. No one else but Mallory would recognize the danger lurking behind those lips. "We're very proud of her."

Mallory cleared her throat in an effort to catch Tori's eye. But Tori wouldn't take the bait. They'd both end up in a fit of laughter.

"Oh, please excuse me, Kathryn," her mother said as if butter wouldn't melt in her mouth. "I see that the mayor and his wife have just arrived. I must go extend my condolences. I'm sure you heard about their poodle, Schmoofy, passing last week."

Kathryn's brows went up, clearly surprised speechless, but they were all spared a reply when Marian headed toward her next victim.

"Don't mind her, Kathryn," Mallory said, idly watching their mother sashay away. "She's had her hair dyed one too many times."

"Mallory," Tori murmured and gave her an elbow to the ribs.

Kathryn tried to hide a smile and briefly looked the other way.

"May I get either of you a drink?" Mallory asked. "I'm heading to the bar."

Tori winced. She'd hoped her sister would hold off longer. "I'll have a Perrier."

"That sounds good to me, too, if you don't mind," Kathryn said.

"Back in a minute."

As soon as Mallory was out of earshot, Tori asked, "How's Beth doing?"

"She's meeting with a divorce attorney tomorrow. A friend of mine who does pro bono work."

"No kidding. That's terrific. Did she actually ask to talk to an attorney?"

"I wouldn't have hooked her up with one if it hadn't been her idea."

Tori sighed. "Of course."

Kathryn smiled. "Don't beat yourself up. When we first start this kind of hands-on volunteering we all want to rush to the rescue."

"I'm honestly trying to keep my distance."

"I know." Kathryn patted her arm. "I wasn't just blowing smoke at your mother. You've been really helpful. Some volunteers read a book while they wait for the hot line to ring. You almost single-handedly got out every invitation and made—"

"Don't, Kathryn. I don't like talking about it. I'd rather you didn't say anything about my work at the center to anyone."

"Why?"

Tori shrugged. "It's...personal."

Alarm flashed in Kathryn's eyes. "I didn't know you felt that way."

"It's no big deal. It's just, I don't know...not

something I normally talk about." Tori glanced around and spotted her mother busy with the mayor. "So Beth doesn't have to worry about attorney's fees, right? Because I could—"

"I promise, it's completely taken care of. My friend has handled quite a few cases for women who've stayed at the shelter. I prepare all the paperwork for court and she files. Her time spent is cut in half."

"Nice." Tori smiled at her. "I've read some of your case workups. You should have been an attorney yourself."

Kathryn laughed. "I was."

"What?"

"I didn't like it."

"Here you go, ladies." Mallory approached with two glasses of sparkling water topped with wedges of lime.

"Thanks." Kathryn accepted one. "Hate to drink and run but I've got to go make nice and mingle. Maybe I can get a few more checkbooks to open." She smiled at Mallory. "Stop by the center some time. Give me a shot at talking you into volunteering."

Mallory chuckled as Kathryn walked out of earshot. "I like her. I doubt I'll volunteer, but I like her."

Tori watched Kathryn cross the room and greet an elderly couple, big-time Houston philanthropists whose names momentarily escaped Tori. She was still too taken aback over what Kathryn had said. Not that it was a big deal. People changed careers all the time. But to go through all those years of law school and then give it up...

"Hey, you." Mallory nudged her. "Did I tell you how great you look in that dress?"

Tori glanced down at the slinky black silk that ended three inches above her knees. "Not too tight?"

"Hell, no. It's perfect, bitch."

"Thank you," Tori said, laughing and then quickly sobered when she spotted her mother heading toward them. "Oh, no."

Mallory followed her gaze and sighed. "And you wonder why I drink? I guess it's time for me to go find Richard."

"Don't you dare leave me." Tori glared at her, and then transferred her gaze back to her mother. She'd stopped to talk with someone, that practiced smile in place, the one that oozed charm and civility and hid any uncharitable thoughts.

Tori had to admit there was more animation in her mother's expression than normal, which made her curious about her mother's companion. Dark hair, dressed in a tuxedo like all the other men in the room, his back was to Tori so she didn't recognize him. He was tall and broad-shouldered like Jake, and if she didn't know better she would have guessed the stranger was him.

JAKE TOOK GREAT PLEASURE in the fact that Mrs. Whitford had no idea who he was. If she had, she wouldn't have wasted so much as a second on him. It didn't matter that he'd been in her garden five days running, that they'd had discussions about her precious roses. She wouldn't know him from Adam.

"I don't believe I've seen you at one of these functions before," she said, accepting a glass of champagne from a passing waiter without a glance or thank you.

He smiled. "I usually just send a check."

"Yes, of course." She returned the smile, leaning toward him and lowering her voice as if in conspiracy. "I know what you mean. I'd often prefer to do the same but, well, as you know, there are times when appearances count."

He sipped his champagne and pretended to be interested in her drivel while he scanned the room. He hadn't seen Victoria yet. She was probably hiding from her mother. Man, two women couldn't be more different. Even in the looks department. Mallory appeared more like her mother, blond and petite, perfect hair, perfect makeup. Not like Victoria.

Thinking of how she looked when she woke up in the morning made him smile. Her hair tangled, faint smudges under her eyes because she admittedly was too lazy to remove all her makeup. Even when she ran out to the market she didn't worry about her hair and slapping stuff on her face. She just went. And she always looked great.

Damn her.

He should still be pissed. In fact, he was angry.

Angry at her for rubbing it in that she still dated other men. More appropriate men. And even angrier at himself for being such a brainless jerk. How could he possibly still want her? Yet, there it was.

"Nice meeting you." Mrs. Whitford extended her hand, annoyance flickering in her eyes. His mind had wandered and she probably felt dissed. "I'm Marian by the way. Marian Whitford."

He accepted her hand. No surprise it was one of those limp, insincere handshakes. "Jake."

"I must run. I see that the Radcliffs have arrived and I need to speak with Eleanor." She was off like a shot, preying on someone more important.

As he surveyed the room again, Jake took another gulp of champagne. The stuff wasn't bad but he'd still rather have beer or wine. He tried to loosen his tie by sticking a finger between it and his shirt but the sucker was too snug.

If this was the way rich people spent their weekends, he just didn't get it. The music wasn't bad, the booze and food actually pretty damn good, but the air kisses and phony smiles were enough to make him gag.

No, thanks. He'd rather sit home with a pizza and a six-pack. Better yet would be sitting on his deck with Victoria, watching the sunset.

Shaking his head, he headed for the bar. If he had any pride, an ounce of common sense, he'd leave. Right now. Before she saw him.

Yeah, right.

"OH, MY, GOD." Mallory's eyes widened. "You're never going to guess who's here."

Tori had traded her Perrier for champagne. At her sister's words, she clutched the crystal so tightly it was a wonder it didn't shatter. Mallory didn't have to tell her who the surprise guest was. She knew. As if she could feel his heat from across the room. "Jake," she whispered.

Mallory looked at Tori. "You know? Oh, my God, did you invite him?

"Of course not."

"He was just talking to Mother."

"I know." Tori kept her back to him, hoping he wouldn't see her.

"I didn't even think she knew him."

"I didn't, either." Tori struggled for composure. "Maybe she doesn't. Maybe she— I don't know..."

"I'll call him over." Mallory lifted a hand, which Tori promptly yanked back.

"Please, Mall, don't."

"What's wrong with you?"

"I'll explain later."

Mallory's brows drew together as she studied Tori with rabid curiosity. And then her gaze drifted past Tori. "Too late. He's coming this way."

Tori swallowed a gulp of champagne, keeping her back to him, hoping like crazy he hadn't seen her. Coming this way didn't mean *coming this way*.

"Good evening, Victoria."

She briefly closed her eyes, moistened her lips and turned around. "Jake."

He smiled, and then glanced at Mallory, who raptly watched them as if she were anticipating the final play at Wimbledon. "Hi, you're Mallory, right?"

She nodded. "I know who you are. A pleasure to finally meet you."

Tori continued to glare at him but to her sister said, "I think it's time you went to look for Richard."

"He can find me."

"Mallory." She slid her sister a warning look.

"Right." She pressed her lips together but couldn't quite hide the smile. "I think I'll go look for my husband."

Tori barely waited until Mallory was out of ear-shot. "Did you follow me here?"

"Not exactly. No, wait a minute." He made a face, amusement lurking in his eyes. "Technically, the answer to that would be no."

"What are you doing here?"

"Same as you. Supporting a good cause."

A waiter stopped to offer them more champagne, and Tori quickly shut her mouth. She smiled politely at the man, accepted a fresh glass of bubbly Jake lifted off the tray for her, and then as soon as the waiter left, she went back to glaring at Jake. "You weren't invited."

"Sure was."

"I sent out practically all of the invitations my-self. I don't remember your name."

"It went to my company, and since I'm presi-dent—"

"Namely?"

"A-One Landscaping. Ring a bell?"

She thought she recognized it, but that didn't matter. "A-One Landscaping?"

"A catchy name if I do say so myself. Number one, I don't need my name plastered on a sign or a building," he said, and she struggled to hold her tongue. "Number two, it puts me first in the Yellow Pages under landscaping. Old trick, I know, but it works."

She glanced around, pinpointing her mother's location. Her father hadn't shown up yet. He always arrived late to social functions. "You could've told me you were coming."

"I didn't think I was, but since I didn't have anything else to do, I figured what the hell." He looked her directly in the eyes. "Besides, you didn't tell me this was where you were going. In fact, you tell me very little about yourself, Victoria."

"Bull," she said, apparently too loudly because a passing white-haired couple sent her a disapproving look. "I've told you more than I've shared with anyone else. Including my sister."

His gaze narrowed slightly. "I'm honored."

"Never mind," she whispered, and darted a look around.

"I meant that, damn it." The disappointment in his voice got to her. "What's the big deal about me being here? I took a shower. Even brushed my teeth and used deodorant for the occasion."

"Oh, Jake." She sighed, knowing she'd hurt him. "You took me by surprise. That's all. I saw you talking to my mother, and, oh, God..." The champagne was making her dizzy. Or maybe it was fatigue. "What the hell was that conversation about?"

"Not you, if that's what you're worried about."

"What else do you have in common?"

His jaw tightened, and he looked at her with a disdain she'd never seen. Cutting, horrible. Shameful. "Perhaps we were discussing the garden."

She hadn't thought of that. "Were you?"

"No." He took a long deliberate sip of champagne, and she could tell he was trying to keep a rein on his temper.

She hadn't meant to anger or hurt him. But that's what she'd done. Not just tonight. The problem had been escalating all along. From the moment she'd invited him into her life, she'd asked for trouble. He'd become an addiction she couldn't kick. It was all her fault, not his.

"I'm sorry," she said finally. "What you and my mother talked about is none of my business."

"You're damn right."

She sucked in a breath, never having seen him so angry. "Excuse me," she said. "I'll leave. I was inexcusably rude and I apologize."

She turned but his hand on her arm stopped her. "We didn't talk about anything important. She didn't even know who I was."

"She didn't?" Tori sighed and shook her head, not at all surprised.

"So don't worry. I didn't embarrass you or your mother."

She stepped back, momentarily speechless. When she finally found the wherewithal to speak, she said, "Are you kidding? The one I'm embarrassed about is my mother."

# 16

JAKE STARED AT Victoria in disbelief. "*She* embarrasses you?"

"Oh, please. How long have you been working in that garden? And I'm not just talking about the past week or so. I'm talking about when you were a kid. You were out there at least four days a week with your dad, and she doesn't even recognize you?" She briefly closed her eyes and clenched her teeth. "Talk about being self-absorbed. No, that's not true. I mean, it is true, but I'm just going to go ahead and say it. The woman is a snob, and yes, I find it mortifying."

He smiled. "Better keep your voice down."

Her startled gaze swept the room. "They don't know who I'm talking about. Is it warm in here, or is it me?"

Trying to loosen his tie again, he said, "It's warm. But I believe your temperature spiked in the past minute or so."

She sighed. "I know I shouldn't be talking about her like this. She's my mother and I do love her. I just don't always like her."

"I understand completely." His head still reeled from her earlier admission. Was it possible he had it all wrong? That Victoria wasn't ashamed to be seen with the likes of him? "Question?"

She gazed at him over her glass, her brows slowly drawing together in wary anticipation.

"What happens next at one of these things? I'm starving."

She burst out laughing, netting her several stares. "They're passing canapés and shrimp. Haven't you had any?"

"Big deal. You have to take one little canapé or everybody looks at you as if you'd been raised by wolves. Hell, I could've eaten the whole tray."

"Hey, we don't want you eating up too much of our profit."

"Our?" He thought a moment. That's right. He'd been too angry to pick up on the invitation thing before. "Is this where you volunteer? At Safe Haven?"

She blinked, gave a small shrug. "Yeah."

"What do you do there?"

"Anything and everything." She glanced around as her body tensed. The music had died down, the bandleader saying something about taking a break. "You might be in luck. I think they're about to serve dinner."

When her gaze came back to him, she caught him staring. He smiled. "Before I forget to tell you, you look absolutely stunning."

"Right. I haven't slept worth a damn in two nights. The bags under my eyes get any worse and I'll have to buy shoes to match."

"Cute. But you still look gorgeous." The black dress fit her perfectly, molding to every curve, showing off those long beautiful legs.

"Stop looking at me like that," she murmured and took a quick sip of champagne.

He smiled. "Like what?"

"You know."

"Like I could eat you up?"

"Knock it off." She cleared her throat, and then smiled to a white-haired woman who looked like Barbara Bush. Turning back to Jake, she said, "Where are you sitting?"

"I have no idea."

"They should have given you a table assignment when you came in."

"Assigned seating, huh?" He snorted. "Interesting."

"It's not like that. Most companies buy tables for ten and then invite employees or clients to sit with them. Assigning a table is necessary to make sure everyone gets seated."

"Is that what your company did?"

"Of course."

"I don't suppose you have a spare seat?"

Her startled gaze met his. "I don't think so. No, I'm sure we don't."

A thought suddenly struck him. God, he was stupid. "Did you come with a date?"

"No." She frowned as if surprised he'd think otherwise.

"If you did, no problem. I'll back off." He'd lied.

If she were here with someone, it would be a big problem. He couldn't stand seeing her with another guy.

"Jake, I didn't—"

"Victoria?" A woman approached, early fifties, attractive, a diamond the size of a cherry hanging from a chain around her neck. "I've been looking for you."

"Mrs. Hastings, hello." Victoria immediately gestured toward Jake. "This is Jake Conners. Simone Hastings."

"A pleasure." She extended her hand, eyeing him as if she were sizing an opponent, and then switched her attention back to Victoria. "Actually, Todd is the one looking for you. Have you seen him?"

"Not yet." Victoria smiled politely, but Jake didn't miss the hint of annoyance in her voice. "I'll keep an eye out for him."

"Save him a dance, would you, darling? It would make his night."

Victoria just smiled again.

Mrs. Hastings nodded to Jake and then wandered off.

"Shit," he muttered under his breath. "They have dancing at this thing."

She chuckled. "Yes, and everyone is expected to get up."

"No way."

She laughed, the golden specks in her eyes catching the light from the chandelier. Her hair glistened with auburn highlights and her smooth flawless skin made him ache to caress her.

She squinted at him. "You're looking at me like that again."

"Your fault. You have no business being so beautiful."

Her cheeks got pink. "I'm warning you..." she murmured, sliding a look to the right where another couple seated themselves at a nearby table.

"Maybe we should take this outside."

"Not possible."

"My car isn't parked too far away. We could neck in the back seat."

Laughing, she shook her head. "Would you keep your voice down?"

"No one heard."

The crowd started moving toward them to claim their seats. Until now the area had been rather private while people mingled closer to the bars set up in two corners of the room.

"Look, we really have to get to our tables so they can start serving," Victoria said. "There's going to be a short program between salad and the main course and then again before dessert is served. We need to stay on schedule."

"Go ahead. I'll catch up with you later."

She frowned. "What are you going to do?"

"Find my seat."

"Oh. Okay." She hesitated.

"Don't worry about me. Go."

"Hey, you two," Mallory said, as she strolled toward them. "We have an extra seat at our table if you're interested, Jake. Richard's been delayed."

He waited for Victoria to say something, but the panic in her expression told him all he needed to know. The warning look she gave Mallory was icing on the cake.

So he wasn't completely off base. Her mother wasn't the only one Victoria was embarrassed by.

"No, thanks," he said, the relief flooding her face pissing him off even more. She talked a good game about her mother but when it came down to it, she was just as phony as dear old Mom. The fact was, he was good enough for the bedroom, but not for polite company. "I'm not staying for dinner."

"But Jake—"

He didn't wait to hear what Victoria had to say. She'd had her chance to speak up a minute ago. Her silence, her expression, had told him all he needed to know. He was a damn fool for coming. For believing they had a shot at something. No matter how far he'd come, how much money he made, he'd never meet the Whitfords' standards. He'd never be good enough in Victoria's eyes.

"Jake, please wait." She kept her voice low as she caught up to him near the door.

"What for?" He stopped. "Did you change your mind? Want me to sit with you and your folks?"

She blinked, her lips parting and then closing as if she thought better of what she'd been about to say. "That's up to you. I don't care."

"Come on, Victoria. You're a better liar than that."

Her eyebrows rose in indignation. "What's gotten into you?"

"A dose of reality. A big heaping dose."

She stared at him, looking so helpless and re-signed he almost felt sorry for her. "Can we talk later?"

"Nothing to talk about. Go enjoy your dinner." He started to leave again but she touched his arm.

"Please, Jake."

"I don't think you want to cause a scene."

She gave him the satisfaction of withdrawing her hand and casting a furtive look at the people linger-ing at the bar. What an easy mark. All he had to do was point out that she might teeter on her social pe-destal.

Without another word, she preceded him out the door, past a couple of valet parkers playing cards as they waited for customers. She stopped well out of earshot of the young men, and turned around to wait for him.

He thought about heading in the other direction, but that would be childish. "Very smooth, Victoria," he said as he got closer. "No one would have guessed you followed me out here."

"I know I've upset you and I'm sorry."

"Why do you think you've upset me?" he asked, and she frowned. "Seriously, I'd like to know."

She crossed an arm over her chest and rubbed her opposite arm. "I'm not sure."

He issued a short humorless laugh. "You know what? Forget it."

"No, I won't forget it. That's not fair. We need to talk. Just not here."

He noticed one of the pimply-faced valet parkers was straining to listen and Jake guided her further away into the shadows. "That's the point. There's nothing to discuss. I don't belong in your world, Victoria. And the hell of it is, I shouldn't be mad. You never made any bones about the fact that all you wanted from me was sex."

"Yes, in the beginning, but then—" She noisily cleared her throat. "Things changed. The relationship got more complicated."

"Complicated?"

"Yes."

"I'm not following."

She let her head fall back and briefly looked up at the darkened sky, exhaling loudly. And then she met his eyes and said, "At some point I started caring more about you than I should."

The admission gave him pause. Not that it changed anything. "But not enough."

"What do you mean?"

Impulsively he touched her cheek. "We had some great times. You trusted me enough to share some aspects of your life, but when it came down to it, I'm not family approved. I couldn't make the cut."

"You make the problem sound as if it's a social thing. It's not."

He lowered his hand. "Right."

"It's much more complex than that."

"The time we spent at my beach house, there were no complications. No family. No exposure. No interference. We were simply two people, getting to know each other, and, I thought, enjoying the hell out of each other's company. Explain that phenomena."

"I'm not shirking responsibility for what happened. I'd temporarily lost sight of my long-term goal." She frowned. "Wait a minute. *Your* beach house?"

"That's right. Free and clear."

"But I— I don't understand."

Of course she didn't understand. She thought he was small-time, scraping by with a rinky-dink landscape company. "I have a knack for revolutionizing things—tools." He shrugged. "I've sold a couple of patents to Forever Green which made me a few bucks. But that isn't important."

"Really?" She folded her arms across her chest. If he wanted to impress her, he'd be sorely disappointed. Temper sparked in her eyes. "Look how much I've shared with you. About my parents, my job, personal stuff... How much have you told me about yourself? All of a sudden you're talking about patents and—"

"Why is that important? Would that information have made me a better candidate for the Whitfords to consider for their daughter?"

She shook her head, contempt simmering in her eyes. "You deliberately led me to believe otherwise about you. What were you doing? Testing me? Or were you saving the information for later to use for negotiating power? Or shock value?"

"Don't." Her words stung. Not that there was any truth to them... "Don't change the subject."

"The hell I am. This is about us. Assumptions you've obviously made about me. I don't care about your patents or your beach house." She lifted her chin, her gaze holding his. "You want the truth? If I dug deep enough into my trust fund I could buy my own damn beach house. This isn't about how much money you have, or my being a Whitford."

"Of course it is. Don't fool yourself." He stared at her in disbelief. She couldn't be that dense. Or was her denial that strong?

"Not the way you see it. You look at everything in a social context. It's not just about money or material things or social standing. It's about family and generations of people pulling their weight. Yes, I've had exceptional advantages in life, and I owe for it. There are prices to pay for everything, and I've got to pay the piper for everything I've had my whole life. What kind of a person would I be if I simply took, and never gave anything back? The company hasn't just made my life easy, it's given hundreds if not thousands of families the food on their tables, the health care for their children. I have an obligation to continue that legacy, and the only way I can do that is to get with the program."

"What price are *you* willing to pay?" He finally started to get it. He was in way over his head, trying to counter years of brainwashing. "You hate your job."

"It doesn't matter. I'm sorry you don't understand but that's just the way it is."

He'd never been so frustrated in his life. "At the center, as a volunteer, do you counsel the women?"

"Not really." At the change of subject, she seemed confused, defensive. "I answer the hot line and talk to them when they want to talk. That's why I had to come back early from Galveston. It wasn't about my job. I'd made a promise to someone at the center."

Taken aback by some of the information, he hesitated. Still, his point was no less valid. "When you talk to those battered women, what do you tell them? Do you encourage them to return home?"

"Are you crazy? Of course not."

"According to your philosophy, it's all about family. About owing. So they should go back to those low-life sons of bitches who call themselves husbands and fathers because that's just the way it is."

"That's absurd and I resent you equating their unfortunate lives to mine."

"It's absurd that you keep going back for more abuse. You hate your job, and you hate the lifestyle. But you're too afraid to admit it to your parents or find a new path. It's crap but it's familiar crap, and you keep going back. Think about it, Victoria, you're not so different."

Her lower lip quivered slightly. "If I didn't think you were so damn sincere, I'd be really angry about now. Wrong, but sincere."

He had to chuckle at that as he yanked his tie free. The relief was humbling. What the hell had he been thinking? He wasn't the tie and tux type.

She sighed. "I just wish you understood. You still think this is about you, and it isn't. Yes, sometimes this lifestyle does suck. And you'd hate it. I don't have a choice."

"Ah." He smiled. "Now you're telling me you're being selfless and sparing me the unpleasantness of being associated with the rich and famous."

"Forget it."

"Right." He snorted. "Sex was all we were ever about, right?" Reaching into his pocket for his keys, he sighed. "Take care of yourself. Make a better life. Don't shortchange yourself. You do have a choice."

Hurt, angry, confused, Tori watched him walk away. God, she wanted to throw something at him. Why couldn't he understand?

"I'd go after him if I were you."

Tori spun toward her sister's voice. "Where did you come from?"

"I snuck out to have a cigarette and saw you two over here tête-à-tête. What's going on?"

Tori sighed. "Nothing. Since when do you smoke?"

Mallory continued to thoughtfully stare off toward Jake's retreating back. "You're making a mistake."

"Please." Tori waved a hand.

"Look, I've had only one martini and one glass of champagne all night. Don't dismiss me. I'm serious. You blow it with him, and you'll regret it for the rest of your life."

"How much did you hear?"

She shrugged. "Not much. Didn't have to. God, Tori, for the past three weeks you've been glowing. Doesn't take much to figure out Jake's the reason. Even on his best day Richard couldn't make me look the way Jake makes you light up."

Tori cleared her throat. "We've had a drink or two, that's all.

"Yeah, right." Mallory laughed and reached into the neckline of her dress and withdrew a cigarette. "Dad tells me Richard does a hell of a job for the company, though." She lit the cigarette and blew a stream of smoke into the air. "Don't make the same mistake I did."

# 17

"DID YOU FORGET BETH went to court today?" Kathryn entered the office and dragged the chair sitting in the corner across the desk from Tori.

"What?" Tori looked up from the stack of papers she was supposed to file but had yet to alphabetize. "Oh, my God, I did forget. What happened?"

"Well..."

"Wait. Don't sit in that chair. The leg is broken."

Kathryn frowned. "It was fixed, Tori. Day before yesterday. You were here when I replaced the washer and nut, remember?"

"Oh." She exhaled, feeling foolish. "Right. I forgot. Tell me what happened with Beth."

"Are you all right?" Kathryn settled into the chair and peered at Tori with concerned eyes.

She smiled. "Of course."

"You haven't been yourself all week. Ever since the benefit, in fact. I hope you aren't still upset with me for singling you out on the program."

"I was never upset with you for that." Tori hadn't been thrilled about being mentioned, but she'd had more troublesome thoughts to worry about since Saturday night...namely Jake.

Kathryn sighed. "I can tell you I'll never do that again. One of the other two volunteers I listed wasn't overjoyed with the attention, either. I honestly thought it would be nice to recognize those of you who'd gone above and beyond."

"Don't worry about it. It's not a big deal. Tell me what happened with Beth."

"That blowhard husband of hers didn't even bother to show up. Poor Beth was so nervous I thought she was going to either pass out or hyper-ventilate. Every time the courtroom door opened, she just about flew off her seat."

"Did he send a lawyer to represent him?"

"Nope. Just didn't show up, and defaulted. You should have seen Beth. Her back straight as a board, her chin up, she was flying so damn high because he'd actually kowtowed to her." Kathryn grinned. "It was awesome. Today was one of those days that was worth a hundred bad ones."

"Damn, I wish I'd been there." Of course she'd been at work, throwing herself into learning every aspect of the business. She'd absorbed more in one week than she had in the past month. "Hey, what were you doing there? You don't usually attend hearings."

Kathryn sighed. "My friend who was handling Beth's case had a personal emergency. She didn't want to ask for a postponement because she was pretty sure Clyde wouldn't show up. I offered to pitch in. I'm still a member of the bar. I just don't practice."

"Why did you quit?"

"Simple. I wasn't happy."

"But all those years of law school."

Kathryn shrugged. "It's not as if I wasted my time. No one can take away what I learned."

Tori shuddered. "I can't imagine what your family and friends had to say."

"Oh, my mother tried heavy-duty guilt to 'make me see reason.' My husband, or I should say my ex-husband, went ballistic when I told him I was giving up my practice. He thought I'd gone totally crazy." She paused, a thoughtful look on her face.

Tori shifted uncomfortably. This was more personal than they usually got. "I hope you don't think I'm prying."

"No, I was just thinking about how I'd almost allowed his reaction to sabotage me. I started second-guessing myself, wondering if it was just a phase I was going through, but in the end I wasn't satisfied. I had to make a decision. So I asked myself: did I want to be happy?

"Good thing I woke up and smelled the coffee. The stupid son of a bitch left me for his prepubescent secretary. The stupid twit could barely spell law."

Tori laughed.

Kathryn smiled. "I don't mean to sound bitter. I'm really not. It's been four years since I quit and not only have I not regretted it for one second, but I couldn't be happier or more fulfilled with what I'm doing now."

"It shows." Tori thought about it for a moment. "Even when all hell breaks loose around here, you never lose it. You stay calm, keep a smile on your face."

She couldn't say the same about herself. Sometimes it was an enormous effort to smile at the office. Even after she left each day it took a couple of hours to wind down, shake the doldrums.

"Believe me, I don't always feel calm inside. And sometimes I could strangle a few people whose names I won't mention." Grinning, she got to her feet. "But when all is said and done, I wouldn't trade my job for anything. I put on a pot of coffee before I came in here. It should be done. Want some?"

"No, thanks. A soon as I leave here, I'm crawling into bed and sleeping like there's no tomorrow."

"Good. You look tired. In fact, take off now if you want. The phone hasn't rung for three hours."

"I'm fine. Thanks."

As soon as Kathryn left, Tori's gaze went to the phone. Just like it always did when she wasn't distracted enough to keep from thinking about Jake. Wondering if she should call. Wondering if he ever would call again.

No. Better this way, she knew. Whatever they had was over. Great while it lasted, but over. *Finito*. No more worrying about hurting his feelings or letting him down easy. Everything was out in the open, and anyway, he was the one who'd walked.

This was good.

Really.

"DON'T FORGET TO LEAVE my truck keys."

"Why?" Jake had just unloaded the last of the groceries he'd brought to his father.

"Because I'm going to work tomorrow, that's why. You think I should walk?"

"The doctor said to wait until Monday."

"I can't wait. Anyway, I'm fine."

Jake shook his head and started stowing the frozen things in the freezer. "Monday will come soon enough."

"I need to see what kind of mess that garden is in. You think I don't know you haven't been there, that you've been sending that Mexican kid instead."

Jake's temper had about reached its limit. He was tired from lack of sleep and with an off-and-on headache that had lasted three days now. "His name is Hector."

"Not him. I know Hector. Good kid. His cousin isn't worth a damn, though." He tossed his cane aside and sank onto the couch. The springs creaked, grating on Jake's nerves. The house, the furniture, everything was old and worn-out and still his father refused to move.

"Hector has been the one taking care of the Whitfords." Jake frowned. "Did they complain?"

"Nah, Harrison would never do that. I just know that things aren't being looked after like they should. You know Mrs. Whitford has a garden walk coming up. Everything has gotta be in tiptop shape."

"Harrison?" That sounded awfully familiar.

"You know, Mr. Whitford."

"Yeah, I know, but I'd never heard you refer to him by Harrison."

"Normally I don't, except when he and I are alone."

Jake snorted. Right. Like Harrison Whitford had time for someone like his dad. "When is that?"

He frowned at him. "You've been out in the sun too long, boy? He's my boss, isn't he?"

They were both grouchy, his dad from being cooped up for so long, and Jake from smarting over Victoria. Not that he spent every waking minute thinking about her. But she never seemed to be far from his thoughts.

The oddest things reminded him of her. Commercials for shampoo, any shampoo, had the damndest ability to carry her vanilla scent to him. So strong that he could swear she was sitting beside him, watching the tube, which he seemed to be doing a lot of this past week.

"You want to tell me what's wrong, son?"

He finished putting away the canned goods before opening a beer. "You want one?"

"No, I want you to come sit with me."

"Oh, brother."

"What? You can't give your old man a few more minutes of your time?"

Jake sighed and took his beer to the couch. He sat down and put his booted feet up on the coffee table.

His father pushed a mechanics magazine over. "Put your feet on this."

Jake stared at the badly scarred wood. No shine. Couldn't even see the grain anymore. He shook his head but did as his father asked.

After a lengthy silence, his dad said, "We used to be able to talk, son. I wish you'd tell me what's wrong."

Jake stretched his neck out from side to side, trying to loosen the tension. "It's this place. You still working for the Whitfords. You don't need the money anymore. I don't get it."

"I should have known better than to ask for your help with the garden."

"What's that supposed to mean?"

"You haven't been on your high horse and bugging me about quitting for some time now. This damn back of mine has got you thinking again."

"Listen to yourself, Pop. *The garden.* You always refer to it like that, as if it's the damn be all and end all."

"That job has been a godsend to me."

Jake sighed and took a swig of beer. "Here we go again."

"Now, you listen to me. You're not some hot-headed kid anymore who used to gripe because someone next door had more toys than you did."

"I never complained about not having—"

"Figure of speech, son," he said, holding up a silencing hand. "I only meant you always had a burr up your butt about the Whitfords, and part of that is my fault. I know now that you don't tell a kid that something is off-limits without a reason and not expect him to feel resentment.

"The truth is, this was a tough neighborhood for you and your sister to grow up in. All these big mansions and fine cars...if it hadn't been the Whitfords, it would've been someone else irritating you."

Jake thought about that for a moment. He had to admit he'd had more than one scrape with kids at school defending his old beat-up VW bus. He'd been so proud of the way he'd fixed it up and they'd laughed in his face.

"But the thing was, after your mother died, I couldn't have found a more ideal job. Not only did it provide a home nearby, but you kids could come see me after you got home from school. I'd know you weren't out carousing. I could give you small jobs in the garden to keep you busy and out of trouble, and manage to keep an eye on you."

Jake hadn't considered those perks. "But, Pop, it's been a long time since sis and I needed baby-sitting. You don't have to keep this job."

"That's the other side of the coin." He smiled. "I love what I do. I love making plants and flowers grow. It's not work to me."

"Fine. We'll buy you a house with enough yard for a small garden. You can putter all you want."

"You think I'd trade what I have for some small patch of land that would bore me in three days?"

"That's the thing, Pop," Jake said gently, mindful of his father's pride. "The garden isn't yours. No matter how much sweat you pour into it, or how many awards the roses win, it's not yours."

"You're wrong. Mrs. Whitford may stand up and

accept the applause and ribbons, but that garden is still mine." Eyes twinkling, he chuckled. "You come by your hardheadedness honestly, son. When I was younger I was just like you. Almost quit a year after I started. I could've strangled that damn Marian Whitford."

"No kidding." His reply had been casual but his reaction was anything but. Jake had never heard a negative word about the Whitfords leave his father's mouth.

"The garden had made the cover of one of those magazines she's so fond of, thanks to me, and all of a sudden she was an expert. She'd come out with her big hat and gloves, not that she ever so much as stuck her little finger in the dirt, and start telling me how to prune and where to plant and how much fertilizer to use."

Jake couldn't help laughing. The old man had gotten worked up just thinking about it.

"Made me so damn mad I called Harrison up that night and told him if that blasted woman ever came near me again I'd hand her my shovel and pruning shears and I was outta there."

Jake shook his head. Hard to imagine his mild-mannered father speaking up like that. "What did he say?"

"He brought over a twelve-year-old bottle of Scotch that night and we drank a good third of it, and then we made a deal. He said she'd never set foot in the garden as long as I was on the grounds. I could plant what I wanted, where I wanted." His lips

curved in a mischievous grin. "Seems she was a real
pain in the ass and as long as she was socializing
with those garden club people she stayed off his
back."

"Harrison Whitford actually sat here in this house
and drank with you."

"That wasn't the only time, either. Sometimes he
stopped on his way home from work. Still does occasionally. Nice fellow."

Jake felt as if he'd stepped into a parallel uni-
verse. None of what his father had said seemed real.
He sat, totally speechless for a few minutes and then
asked, "Did you ever tell him about Victoria?"

His father's gaze narrowed. "What about her?"

"How she'd run away and you picked her up."

He frowned. "How would you know about that?"

Jake finished off his beer. He shouldn't have
brought her up. The old man didn't need to know
about Jake seeing her.

"Did she tell you about it?" Leaning back against
the cushions, he frowned speculatively at Jake. "Had
to be her. I never told a soul."

"Yeah, she told me."

"When?"

Jake muttered a curse that earned him an annoyed
look. "A couple weeks ago."

"Didn't know you'd seen her. I believe she just
got home from school about two months ago."

Jake didn't say anything. He thought about getting another beer, but he had to drive. In fact, it was
time he headed back to his apartment.

"Yep, I sure felt bad for that kid." His father shook his head. "Sure made me feel less guilty about you kids not having a mother. Here she had both and I never saw a little girl more lonely and scared."

"Victoria? Scared?"

His father eyed him with curiosity. "She didn't think she fit in. Thought she was adopted and unwanted because she didn't like to do the things her mother wanted her to do. Like I said, Harrison is a nice enough fellow, but as a father, I don't think he's worth a damn. There was no reason for that bright, pretty little girl to think she wasn't good enough."

Jake's gut clenched. His thoughts swirled back to conversations they'd had at the beach. To memories of her as a kid standing at the window, looking lonely and miserable. Was that what Victoria was still trying so desperately to do? Fit in?

"I had to practically drag her back home. She kept begging to stay here. Nearly broke my heart."

Jake cleared his throat. He had to get out of here. Be by himself for a while. "Well," he said getting to his feet, "seems she turned out okay."

"You leaving?"

"Yeah, I have stuff to do."

"Thanks for the groceries, son. And don't forget to leave my truck keys."

Jake sighed, and dug the keys out of his pocket. "On one condition. Hector goes with you tomorrow."

After a resentful frown, his father's mouth slowly curved. "Why don't you go with me?"

No way could he show up there. "I'm gonna be busy."

"Think about it."

"See you, Pop."

He got out the front door and lingered on the front steps for a moment, took a deep breath and tried to clear his head. Tried to shake the feeling he'd been run over by a steamroller.

By the time he'd driven the twenty minutes it took to get to his apartment, his thoughts were in such turmoil it felt as if he'd run a marathon.

He went straight to the refrigerator, got a beer and headed for the couch—almost new, made from fine Italian leather. Most of his furniture was contemporary, expensive. He bought what he liked without regard for trend or price.

His apartment was okay, two bedrooms but small in a moderately nice neighborhood. He'd never once asked Victoria here. Not because he'd thought she'd turn him down, he realized. He'd been afraid she might've accepted the invitation.

That steamed him. It was a perfectly nice place. Good enough for him even though he could now afford better. Jeez, why did he have to gauge everything in his life by her standards?

He swung his feet up onto the couch and took a gulp of beer.

Damn good question.

# *18*

TORI STOOD at her bedroom window gazing out at the melon-colored roses that bordered the gazebo steps. Every time she looked outside, she swore she found a new favorite.

"Mind if I come in?"

She turned to see Mallory standing in the doorway. "Only if you brought chocolate."

Her sister grinned. "As a matter of fact—"

"No way."

Mallory walked in, laughing, two small fun-size packages of peanut M&M's in her hand.

"You've got to be kidding. Is that all?"

"They're both for you."

"Sheesh."

"You ingrate." Mallory dropped both small bags in Tori's hand. "I had to mug two trick-or-treaters for these."

"I apologize. You're the best sister in the world." Tori sighed and tore open one of the bags, at the corner, so she could dump the candies directly into her mouth.

Mallory went to the window and looked out. "He hasn't been here all week."

"I didn't figure he would be. You want some of these?"

"No, thanks. Have you tried calling him?"

"Of course not. Why would I do that?"

Mallory snorted and turned away from the window. "And they say you're the brighter sister."

"No one says that."

"Come on, *everyone* says that. Not that I care. I proved I'm smarter. You don't see me going to the office every day."

Tori laughed. It felt good. She hadn't done that much during the past week. And then she sighed and popped a couple more M&M's into her mouth. "Where's Richard?"

"I have no idea." Mallory sat on the edge of her bed and bounced a few times. "You need a new mattress."

"That's Mother's problem. I'm moving out in two weeks. I signed a lease for an apartment last night."

"Damn it. I can't believe you told her without me being there."

"Chill out. I haven't told her yet."

"Oh." Mallory smiled. "Good. The day's looking up."

Tori sat next to her sister. "How's your house coming?"

"Richard thinks we'll be able to move in by the tenth. Of course he'll be gone again. Hong Kong this time, I think. So I'll have to coordinate everything."

"How can you stand him being gone so much? Can't Dad send someone else sometimes? Richard can't be that indispensable."

"I don't mind that he's gone. Really. I've just re-joined Junior League. I'll have plenty to do."

Tori stared at her sister, not a trace of resentment or unhappiness in Mallory's face, and Tori finally got it. Mallory had turned into their mother. Not the snobby part, but she'd traded happiness and love for financial freedom and social standing. The truly sad part was her growing indifference.

"Come on, Tori. Quit looking at me like that." Mallory nudged her with a shoulder. "It's not as if I'm unhappy, per se."

"Do you love Richard?"

"Yes, in my own way. I know I don't feel the pas-sion toward him as you do with Jake, but he's a de-cent man and he works hard and—"

"Don't bring Jake into this."

"Somebody has to. Christ, don't be such a twit." Mallory got up. In a lower voice she said, "I need a cigarette." She got to the door. "Just call him. You couldn't have solved a damn thing standing outside the Four Seasons. Call him. Even if it's just for clo-sure."

Tori waited until she'd disappeared and then fell back on her bed and stared at the ceiling. She laughed humorlessly, realizing how freely they'd spoken, the bedroom door open, and Mother lurk-ing God knows where.

And then the word *closure* echoed in her head and

she bit her lip, her eyes getting annoyingly misty. Was that all she wanted from him? Was she that big a coward? Did she want to end up like Mallory? Resigned. Indifferent. Sneaking cigarettes.

Tori briefly closed her eyes. Her sister was an adult. As nasty a habit as smoking was, it was still her choice. She didn't have to hide it. Screw Mother or Richard or anyone else who didn't approve.

The thought jolted Tori and she sat up as realization hit her with the force of a tidal wave. What about her choice? She had one. She'd told Jake she didn't. She'd been furious over his comparing her to a battered woman. So furious she hadn't gotten the message.

But in concept, he was right. She didn't like her job. And she hated the way her mother manipulated dinners in order to showcase suitable men, at least men her mother found appropriate. Men Tori normally wouldn't have more to do with than polite conversation. Yet she stuck around to be subjected over and over again.

Maybe Kathryn had a point that day she'd implied Tori might be throwing too much of herself into Beth's problems as a way for Tori to avoid her own. Kathryn hadn't actually come out and said that's what she thought Tori was doing. She was far too smart. Tori's defenses would have risen so quickly the message would have been lost forever.

God, but she admired and envied Kathryn. The

woman had given up so much. But she'd made the decision and never looked back.

Tori's pulse rate accelerated. Kathryn's words had haunted her for days. She wanted to be happy, too. That couldn't be asking for too much. Didn't she deserve happiness?

Hands shaking, she got out her laptop.

To: The Gang at Eve's Apple
From: Angel@EvesApple.com
Subject: xxx
Hi, Guys. I know I haven't written for a week. Lots of stuff has happened, including a big blowup with Jake (yes, that's his real name). By the way, my name is Victoria (Tori) Whitford. I live in Houston and I'm probably the biggest coward and idiot this side of the Mississippi.

I lied. It wasn't just about sex with Jake. That probably lasted only till the second time I was with him. I fell hard. I got scared because he didn't fit into my plan. I finally figured out that I've never had a plan. My parents had one for me. One I've always despised. But I've been too big a chicken to admit it even to myself.

After I write and send this e-mail, I'm going to call Jake. If he doesn't answer his phone, I'm going to drive to his father's house and get his address. Whether he likes it or not, we are going to talk. Which will hopefully evolve into something else after I tell him how much I love and adore him.

<<Big sigh>> I feel better already.

I love you guys, too. Next time I write I hope it's with really good news.

Love,

Tori.

She reviewed the e-mail, and then went back and deleted her last name. This was therapeutic enough without her blabbing everything. She hit Send, closed her laptop and grabbed her purse. The doorbell rang as she got near the top of the spiral staircase, so she rerouted herself toward the servants' stairs that led to the kitchen.

Just as she left the last step, she heard her mother calling to her. Tempted as she was to ignore her and slip out the back door, Tori moved closer to the hallway to listen. She never had visitors.

Her heart raced. Was that Jake's voice?

"I'm sorry. Apparently she isn't in," she heard her mother say, and Tori hesitated only long enough to take a deep steadying breath.

"I'm here," she said, and hurried into the foyer.

"Oh." Her mother looked from her back to Jake, giving him an icy stare.

He wore jeans, not too faded, and a black polo shirt, along with his ever-present cowboy boots.

"Hey." She smiled.

"Hi, Victoria."

"Come in."

Her mother stepped back to allow Jake entrance.

She squinted at him. "You were at the dinner last weekend."

"Yes, how are you Mrs. Whitford?"

"I know you..." she said, frowning in confusion.

"You should," Tori said, gesturing for Jake to follow her. "His father has worked here for over twenty years. He's practically part of the family." At her mother's appalled look, she tried not to laugh. "Don't you have a brunch to go to?"

Her brows rose in indignation, and then her gaze fell pointedly to the purse and keys Tori still held in her hand. Tori met Jake's eyes and said, "I had an errand to run. But he's here."

His lips slowly started to curve into that wonderful sexy smile she'd missed all week. She couldn't take her eyes off him.

"Sorry I dropped by without calling," he said.

"That's okay. Mother was just leaving." She smiled at her mother who brusquely tucked her purse under her arm and headed for the door. "Let's go into the library."

She led the way, unbelievably nervous knowing he was right behind her. She had so much to tell him, and she had no idea how he'd take it. The fact that he was here at all was a good sign.

Wasn't it?

Panic overtook good sense. Maybe he'd seen her name on his caller ID and had come to tell her to stop bothering him. Or maybe he wanted to go back to having no-strings-attached sex. The thought stung.

She preceded him into the library and swallowed hard. No more being a coward. She'd tell him exactly what she wanted. And if he laughed in her face, then she'd just have to accept the rejection and humiliation.

He closed the door behind them, and anxious to say her piece, she turned around. Before she could open her mouth, his arms slid around her.

"Do you have any idea how much I've missed you?" he whispered, his warm minty breath dancing across her chin.

"Oh, Jake. I have so much to say to you."

"It can wait." He kissed her, gently at first, his hunger growing until she finally had enough wits to pull away.

She struggled for breath. "No, it can't."

He drew his head back in surprise, but keeping her in his arms, stared, waiting for her to continue.

"I don't want it to be about sex anymore."

His gaze narrowed slightly.

"I want to see you. I want to see if we have something going. I want—" She swallowed hard. "I love you, and if you can't handle that, then you need to tell me now."

He grinned. "If you could only be that forceful with your father about your job you'd—"

She shoved at his chest. "I just told you the most important news of my entire life and you're talking about my father."

He pulled her close again, and she had to tilt her head back to look at him. "It's news to you. Not me."

"What?"

"We both fell in love at the beach. But we were too stubborn or scared to take the next step."

"We did?"

"Deep down, don't you know that?" He smiled and touched the tip of her nose. "You were right about me. I made a lot of assumptions about you. Most of them wrong."

"You weren't alone."

"A small consolation." He winced. "That night at the dinner when your mother asked why she hadn't seen me at other functions, I told her I usually just send a check. Which is true. And she gave me this knowing wink and said how she preferred to do the same. I didn't think much about it until I saw your name on the program later." He shook his head. "Hell, you're in there getting your hands dirty, and really making a difference."

"Hey, stop it."

"I admire that, Victoria. I admire you for stepping in. You don't sit in your ivory tower."

She looped her arms around his neck. "I admire the way you kiss me. But the memory is getting a little fuzzy it's been so long."

One side of his mouth went up before he met her lips, slowly nibbling and tasting, making her knees weak.

Finally, she was the one who retreated. "Question?"

He raised his brows.

"Where do you see yourself a month from now?" she asked, not quite ready to ask the tough question.

"Hmm...let's see..." He frowned, but a grin tugged at the corners of his mouth. "The beach house. It might be a little cold but we'll have a fireplace."

Her heart lifted.

"What about you?" His gaze held hers.

"Well, I'm not sure. After I have a talk with my father, I may be unemployed."

"Not for long." Respect gleamed in his eyes. "Not a bright lady like you."

She moistened her lips. "Scary stuff."

"I'll be with you all the way."

"I know," she whispered. "I know."

# _Epilogue_

_One year later_

"ARE YOU SURE we should be doing this?" Jake stared at the glittering neon sign with misgiving.

Tori gaped at him. "You don't want to get married?"

"Of course I do." He slid an arm around her shoulders. "But I don't know about doing it like this." He frowned again at the flashing sign of the True Blue Wedding Chapel. "Hell, I think your mother is just starting to like me. This is gonna really piss her off."

"Coward."

"Damn right. She doesn't pull any punches."

Tori laughed and hugged him closer.

"Seriously, she's gone through a lot of trouble making arrangements with the caterers and florists and having invitations sent out. And what about Mallory? She even canceled her last trip with Richard to help with the preparations."

Tori leaned her head on his shoulder. "She's so much happier now that Richard is spending more time at home and she's occasionally traveling with him. I'm proud of her for speaking up and telling him what she needed." She sighed. "Okay, we'll have the reception the family wants, but we'll get married our own way. Even if it is at a tacky Las Vegas wedding chapel."

"Fair enough." He smiled. He was so damn proud of her. No one walked over Victoria Whitford. Not even him. Even her mother tended to tread lightly these days, making suggestions instead of demands.

And the family business was doing just fine without her. But she was still on the board and attended monthly meetings, but her days and energy were spent at the center.

"Jake?"

"Hmm?"

"Do you mind getting married here?" This time she frowned at the gaudy flashing blue and purple neon.

"Honey, I love you. I'd marry you anywhere."

She tilted her head back and smiled at him. "You know something?"

He smiled back, knowing what was coming. It was their private routine. "What?"

"I love you, too." She broke away and then took his hand. "Ready?"

"Come on." He led her toward the door. "But we're still going to Disneyland for our honeymoon."

"You got it."

Laughing like two giddy teenagers, they entered the chapel.

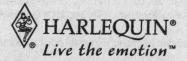

## HARLEQUIN

# Temptation

### is turning twenty!

## We're young, we're legal (well almost) and we're old enough to get into trouble!

And to celebrate our coming-of-age, we're reintroducing one of our most popular miniseries.

Whenever you want a sassy, sexy book with a little something out of the ordinary, look for...

# Editor's Choice

**Don't miss July's pick...**

# I SHOCKED THE SHERIFF
## by MARA FOX

When Roxy Adams shows up in her bright yellow Porsche, Sheriff Luke Hermann knows he and his small Texas town will never be the same. Within twenty-four hours, he's pulled her out of a catfight, almost hauled her off to jail and spent the most incredible moments of his life in her bed. But Luke knows she'll love him and leave him soon enough. Still, before she does, he intends to make sure she'll miss being held in the long arms of the law....

*Available wherever Harlequin books are sold.*

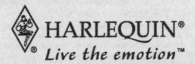

If you enjoyed what you just read,
then we've got an offer you can't resist!

# Take 2 bestselling
# love stories FREE!

# Plus get a FREE surprise gift!

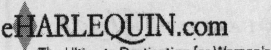

## HARLEQUIN® *Blaze*™
## HARLEQUIN® *Temptation*®

# Single in South Beach

### Nightlife on the Strip just got a little hotter!

Join author Joanne Rock as she takes you back to Miami Beach and its hottest singles' playground. Club Paradise has staked its claim in the decadent South Beach nightlife and the women in charge are determined to keep the sexy resort on top. So what will they do with the hot men who show up at the club?

### GIRL GONE WILD
*Harlequin Blaze #135*
*May 2004*

### DATE WITH A DIVA
*Harlequin Blaze #139*
*June 2004*

### HER FINAL FLING
*Harlequin Temptation #983*
*July 2004*

Don't miss the continuation of this red-hot series from Joanne Rock!
*Look for these books at your favorite retail outlet.*

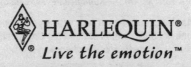